Mission: Impossible?

Name: Daniel D'Artois, aka "the Prince of Paris"

Height: 6'1"

Hair: Thick and luscious

Eyes: Strictly bedroom

Home: Paris, France (duh)

Background: Son and heir of Alain D'Artois, owner and head designer of Vedette, the hottest fashion house in France.

Your Mission (Should You Choose to Accept It): Daniel would be a jewel in any girl's crown. Use your womanly wiles to capture his heart. This is an assignment of international importance! Relations between France and America have never been colder. It's up to you to bridge the gap.

Also by Gillian McKnight

To Catch a Prince

The Frog Prince

Gillian McKnight

Simon Pulse
New York • London • Toronto • Sydney

To Corinna Cappetti-Klein

SIMON PULSE
An imprint of Simon & Schuster Children's Publishing Division
1230 Avenue of the Americas, New York, NY 10020
Copyright © 2006 by Watermark Productions
All rights reserved, including the right of reproduction in whole or in part in any form.
SIMON PULSE and colophon are registered trademarks of Simon & Schuster, Inc.
Designed by Steve Kennedy
The text of this book was set in Granjon
Manufactured in the United States of America
First Simon Pulse edition June 2006
10 9 8 7 6 5 4 3 2 1
Library of Congress Control Number 2006922235
ISBN-13: 978-0-689-87735-3
ISBN-10: 0-689-87735-8

One

A Tale of Two Telegrams

When the first fax arrived, Alexis Worth was busily putting the finishing touches on her new bedroom. Technically, it wasn't new. She had slept in this same room as far back as she could remember. The room looked completely different, though, from the way it had a month ago. For most seventeen-year-olds, a redecoration project like this would be a major event. Not for Alexis. She overhauled her room at least twice a year, if not more. This summer, she had chosen an all-white theme: crisp white cotton sheets, a snowy duvet, sheer curtains, and a shaggy natural rug. The antique bed frame, dresser, and nightstands looked fresh and new, thanks to several coats of ivory enamel.

Unfortunately, in keeping with last winter's Christmas theme, the walls had been poinsettia red. It took two coats of primer and six layers of paint to cover them, but at last they were as fresh and virginal as Alexis intended. Well, maybe virginal wasn't the right word. Peaceful. Meditative. Restful. Yes, that was the effect she was going for.

After spending a hectic holiday season in Aspen with her family, Alexis had decided to simplify her life. No more late-night parties that left her feeling tired and cranky. No more midnight raids on the refrigerator that took a toll on her hips. And no more flirting with boys. *Especially* no more flirting with boys.

So when she saw a photo in a magazine of an all-white meditation room with an accompanying article on Zen Buddhism called "Purify Your Life," Alexis sprang into action. Down came the photographs of family and friends that crowded the walls. Up went a single Japanese scroll with a peach blossom painted on it and a haiku printed underneath. (Never mind that she couldn't read Japanese—the characters *looked* soothing.) Fringed lamps were replaced by paper lanterns. A mirrored vanity table, once loaded with cosmetics, was now cleared of everything but an incense burner, a silver handbell, and a fat white candle. The cosmetics only went as far as the first two drawers of the vanity, where they were packed so tightly, it was hard to close the drawers, but Alexis figured she would deal with insides later; right now, she was worried about surfaces. On a piece of white parchment she hand-lettered the words "The end to suffering can only come through wisdom and compassion" and taped it to the mirror.

She was just arranging a vase of white roses on her

nightstand when Helene came in and flopped down onto the bed. Helene was many things—outgoing, enthusiastic, energetic—but she was definitely not restful. There were more colors in her hair (pink, with darks tips and light roots) than there were in all of Alexis's bedroom. Still, Alexis loved her more than anybody else in the world. Not only was Helene her stepsister, she was also her best friend.

Best friends can be bossy with each other, though, so when Alexis barked, "No shoes allowed!" Helene merely rolled her eyes and yanked off her combat boots, throwing them in the corner. As usual, she wore a hodgepodge of clothes that would have looked crazy on anyone else: a lime green camisole, a bright orange pencil skirt, and purple patterned tights. Plus chipped red nail polish. And of course the hair. Alexis's all-white oasis was suddenly a riot of color.

"Here's something to go with your color scheme," Helene said. "Take a look at this." She threw a balled-up piece of paper toward her sister. It landed on the white carpet and nearly vanished into the background.

"Would it kill you just to hand it me?" Alexis groused as she leaned to retrieve the paper. Smoothing it out, she saw it was a fax. From Paris. From Helene's father, no less. *Miss you loads. Come and visit this summer. Ticket to follow. All love, Dad.* Sensing trouble, Alexis frowned.

"What made him contact you now, of all times? It's not like he's ever asked you to come visit before."

Helene groaned. "He just got married. My guess is he wants me to meet my new stepmother. You know, to prove what a happy, healthy family we really are."

Alexis nodded sympathetically. On the surface, the girls didn't have much in common, but they did share one important thing: They had survived their parents' divorces and the remarriages that followed. Almost nine years ago, Alexis's father, Hugo Worth, had married Helene's mother, Brenda Masterson. And even though the girls were grateful to have a stable home life, their family troubles were far from solved.

Helene's dad, Trevor Masterson, was a busy Hollywood screenwriter. A year ago he had moved to Europe, claiming he needed to get away from the crass commercialism of the American film industry. When she was little, Helene and her father had been very close. He had recorded every phase of her growth on video; her finger paintings were displayed in gilded frames in his office. After his career took off, he was suddenly too busy for his family. Helene's parents divorced. Even now, with him working "outside the Hollywood rat race," her father's schedule was still too crowded to accommodate summer visits. Christmas break was out of the question—that was rewrite season. The last time they had seen each other had been three days after Helene's sixteenth birthday. It had been a disaster.

They'd arranged to meet in New York City to see *The Nutcracker*. Helene knew it was corny, but it reminded her of when her parents were still together. They'd gone every year, and she wasn't about to refuse when her dad called to invite her. He was in the city for just a couple of days, he said, but he'd managed to snag box seats. She accepted with enthusiasm and kept to herself how mad she was that they hardly got to see each other anymore.

She arrived at Lincoln Center a half hour early, pink-cheeked at the anticipation of meeting him. When she spotted her father approaching the fountain outside of Lincoln Center, she stood up and waved. At first, Mr. Masterson looked as though he didn't recognize her. Then, as he got closer, he squinted his eyes. "Helene, is that you?"

She laughed and threw her arms around him. "Of course it's me, Daddy. Who else would it be?"

Her father stepped back and surveyed her from head to toe. Helene usually stood out from the crowd, but on this day she had taken careful pains to dress as conservatively as possible. Not only was her hair its genuine color (dirty blond), but she had blown out her tangled curls into soft, feminine waves. She was wearing an elegant scoop-necked black velvet dress her grandmother had sent her for Christmas. True, she had jazzed it up with a skull pin, but by Helene's standards, she looked downright presentable.

"What happened to my little girl?" Mr. Masterson demanded, shaking his head in disbelief. "When I last saw you, you were wearing a Xena Warrior Princess T-shirt and a pair of ripped jeans."

"Dad, I outgrew that shirt about six years ago. Besides, I could hardly wear a T-shirt and jeans to the ballet!"

What did he expect? Helene asked herself as her father looked her up and down. That she hadn't changed at all over the years?

"Don't you think that dress is cut a little low?" he asked a moment later. And then: "And when did you start wearing all that makeup?"

She would have been perfectly happy if he'd just said what a pretty young woman she had grown into, but he didn't. Not once.

The rest of the evening was no more a success. Helene had sat on the edge of her seat, as far away from her father as possible. It was impossible to swallow over the hard, angry lump in her throat. As soon as the final curtain fell, she bolted for the exit and went home on the train. She cried so hard that her makeup ran down her face and ended up on the velvet dress. Not that she'd ever wear it again. Her father had tainted it with his words.

Mr. Masterson, though, was Parent of the Year compared to Alexis's mom. During her divorce, Vanessa Worth hadn't even sought custody of her only child. All she'd asked for was the BMW and hefty alimony payments. Every once in a while, Alexis would receive postcards from far-flung places like Biarritz, Saint-Tropez, or Rio with the same scribbled note: "Having loads of fun. Wish you were here. Love, V."

Helene was probably the only person who fully understood how much Vanessa's behavior hurt Alexis. It would be impossible to make up for all the forgotten birthdays, spoiled holidays, and broken promises that Alexis had suffered at the hands of her mother. Still, the girls were there for each other with comforting hugs and soothing words when their parental troubles became too great for them to bear.

So when she saw the chance to rescue Helene from an entire summer of forced family togetherness, Alexis stepped in. "Summer in Paris? Sounds wonderful. When do we leave?"

Helene sat bolt upright on the bed. "You mean you'll go with me?" she cried, bouncing up with joy. "That would be great. I dread meeting Daddy's new wife. I can't even bring myself to call her my stepmother. Even that term seems too warm and friendly for such an ice queen."

"What makes you think she's an ice queen?"

"Alexis, give me a break! Have you let your subscription to *British Vogue* lapse? Her picture's on the cover this month! 'Margot Morganne: France's New Femme Fatale.' She's as beautiful as Bridget Bardot, and I'm not just talking about her face. The woman can't weigh more than a hundred pounds, and I'll bet a third of it comes from those gigantic boobs of hers. It's bad enough seeing that body on the cover of a magazine. Can you imagine it draped all over my middle-aged father? Disgusting!" Helene flopped back onto the mattress and covered her multicolored head with a white pillow.

Alexis came over and took the pillow away—half to see her sister when she spoke to her, and half to keep it from getting stained with Helene's heavily applied lipstick and mascara. "Helene, my sister, you are simply suffering from a textbook case of daughterly jealousy, further compounded by unreasonably low self-esteem. You know how much airbrushing goes on with those magazine pictures. Besides, Margot's an actress. Those sultry pouts are just part of her image. In real life, she's probably a very nice person."

Helene narrowed her dark-rimmed eyes and looked at Alexis. "Suddenly you're a regular Dr. Phil, so level-headed and reasonable. What's wrong? Feeling okay?"

Alexis gave a gentle smile, the kind you'd give to a hysterical mental patient right before jabbing her with a sedative-filled needle. "Oh, Helene, all that childish behavior is a thing of the past. Now that I've taken up Zen Buddhism, I've decided to stop imposing my will on the universe and accept its natural order instead. We must learn to live in the moment and accept things as they really are. The sooner we do, the sooner we will all attain enlightenment." She leaned to wipe the mascara smudges from Helene's face, discreetly glancing at her pillow to make sure it was unscathed. It was *so* difficult to get Max Factor out of silk organza.

Helene lightly swatted Alexis's hand away from her blackened cheek. "No, leave them. Otherwise, you'll disturb the natural order of the universe. This is going to be some trip! I'm going to meet my movie-star stepmother with my Zen master stepsister. How sophisticated can you get! All that's missing from my entourage is a pet psychic."

"What you need is to make a fresh start, sweetie," Alexis said, folding her legs into the lotus position.

Noting her sister's smooth movements, Helene suspected she must have been practicing. "Well, remember last summer?" she said now, trying to keep her tone nonchalant.

"I seem to remember something about it." Exasperation was creeping into Alexis's soothing, placid voice. She tried to stay calm and neutral, but she couldn't resist an inquisitive "What about it?"

"It's Lazlo," Helene said.

The MasterWorth sisters, as they were sometimes called (especially if someone was telling stories about their adventures) had spent the previous summer in London, where they had met a pair of British boys named Lazlo and Simon. Lazlo was boyish and irreverent, while Simon was shy and gentlemanly, but both were persistent. They'd had to be, because Helene and Alexis were in their "prince phase," as they now called it, and had spent much of the summer nursing an obsession for Prince William. Just in time, the girls had come to their senses and realized that wacky Lazlo was a perfect match for Helene, while sweet Simon was just Alexis's cup of tea. The summer had ended much too soon, with both couples agreeing to separate on friendly terms until they could meet again.

Alexis tried to concentrate on her perfect posture, but her mind was filled with an image of kissing Simon in the back of a London cab as it sped through rainy streets. "What about Lazlo?" she said in the most level voice she could manage.

"Ever since last summer, I haven't been able to get him out of my mind. I know we agreed to see other people once I got home . . . long-distance relationships are such a drag. But since then, I haven't met anyone I like nearly as much." Helene chewed her bottom lip.

Alexis frowned. "Haven't you heard from him lately? I seem to remember the two of you exchanging torrid e-mails just a few months ago."

Helene shook her head. "That's just it. I haven't heard from him in over six weeks. Do you think he's forgotten me?" Her green eyes swam with fresh tears.

Alexis untangled herself from the lotus position and stood up, shaking back her hair and straightening her shoulders. "So what if he has?" It was more of a challenge than a question. "You're seventeen, not seventy. This is your time to go out and experiment. Besides, Lazlo wasn't so great. Remember that weird little bump on his nose? And how his ears stuck out like jug handles? Face it, Helene, he's hardly the prototype for Prince Charming."

At the mention of Lazlo's bumpy nose, Helene assumed a dreamy, faraway expression. "Yeah, he *was* kinda funny looking, wasn't he?" she breathed. Coming from Alexis, "funny looking" was a put-down, but Helene made it sound like the highest of compliments.

Alexis smoothly switched gears. "Well, if it's funny-looking men you want, I hear Paris is teeming with them. Remember the Phantom of the Opera? And the Hunchback of Notre Dame?"

Helene laughed and threw the pillow at Alexis. "Okay, Zen Master Lexy, you've convinced me. Off to

Paris we'll go, wicked stepmother or no. I'll just call Daddy to tell him we're both coming."

"Do you think it'll be a problem?"

"Oh, no. I get the feeling that he's as nervous about this meeting as I am. If it means you'll be a buffer between him and me, he'll say yes."

Just then there was a knock at the door. It was Brenda Masterson, Helene's mom. "Alexis, honey, this fax just came for you. I think it's from your mother." Alexis and Helene looked at each other in alarm. There had to be something very serious for Vanessa to contact her daughter out of the blue. Somebody must be sick, or dead, or . . .

Alexis looked down at the bright white paper and read aloud slowly, *"Miss you loads. Pack your bags and join me in Greece for the summer. It's time we caught up. Love, Mom.'"*

Alexis thought she was managing to look nonchalant— but her skin had gone as white as the walls of her room.

"Nice to see she's finally taken her parental responsibilities seriously," Alexis said. "She usually signs her notes 'Vanessa' instead of 'Mom.' Hmmm . . ." Alexis pondered for a moment. "Maybe it *is* time to catch up after all these years. It could be a healing experience for us both."

Wow, Helene thought. Buddhism really *has* mellowed her. A few weeks ago, this whole room would have been torn to shreds.

Apparently, however, Alexis hadn't quite attained full enlightenment. After a minute's silence, she crumpled the fax in one fist and then ran into the bathroom, locking the door behind her. Loud sobs echoed throughout the bedroom. Helene and her mother exchanged stricken glances.

"Let's give Lexy some privacy," Ms. Masterson whispered, and steered Helene out of the room.

That's the problem with living in the moment, Helene thought as she and her mom made their way to the kitchen. When the moment sucks, there's no escape.

Two

Les Misérables

"Dad, there is absolutely no way that Helene and I can be separated this summer," Alexis said. Her face was freshly scrubbed, but her eyes were still red from crying. "We're both going to Paris. We have to!"

Alexis and her father were seated in Hugo Worth's home office, which smelled of leather, furniture polish, and expensive cigars. The walls were covered with framed photographs of Alexis's dad with various celebrity clients. Normally, Alexis would have studied the walls to see if any new stars had been added. Today, however, she barely glanced at the pictures of Jude, Orlando, and Usher. All her attention was focused on Mr. Worth, who—despite Alexis's assertion that there was "no way" she and Helene could be separated this summer—still had the final say on her vacation plans.

If you didn't know Alexis's father, you'd never guess he was a high-powered public relations executive. He looked more like a personal trainer. His bright blue eyes were only a shade darker than his daughter's, with warm laugh lines around the edges. Alexis loved him tremendously, although she was very careful when and how she expressed that. It was important to let your parents think they had to *earn* your love, that the smallest wrong move on their part and you might despise them forever. The barest hint was usually enough. This was especially important to remember during times like these, when you had to spin a story a certain way.

Unfortunately, Alexis was employing this tactic with the very man who had taught it to her. Mr. Worth smiled and shook his head. He walked around the desk and took Alexis's hands in his.

"Look, Alexis, there's no point arguing. This summer, Helene's going to Paris to visit her father, and you're going to Greece to visit your mother."

Alexis began to protest, but Mr. Worth plowed ahead. "Yes, I know I risk being brought up on charges of cruelty and neglect by shipping you off to Europe. After all, most girls your age would be busy working jobs during the summer. I'm forcing you to give up an entire summer of saying 'May I interest you in a super-combo deal' or even the awe-inspiring 'Do you want fries with that?' Instead, I'm condemning you to spend two whole months sailing around the Mediterranean on a yacht. It's a wonder Child Services isn't knocking on the door right now."

Alexis scowled. "I'd rather make license plates in some dingy little cell than be forced to make small talk with Vanessa. The last time I visited her, I ended up spending all my time with the maid while she busied herself flirting with the new tennis pro at the club."

Mr. Worth's expression darkened. "Alexis, please. Don't call your mother 'Vanessa.' She deserves some respect. I know your relationship hasn't always been easy, but I think you owe it to yourself to work on it."

Alexis's eyes flashed. "You mean I owe it to you not to bring any negative publicity to your firm. After all, it wouldn't do for a man in your position to be accused of withholding visiting privileges from his ex-wife."

Alexis's father winced. "That's not fair, Lexy, and you know it. The divorce was ugly, and I'm sorry for that. At the time, your mother and I were more focused on hurting each other than on doing what was best for you. But now that you're old enough to take control of the situation, couldn't you be a little nicer to your mother?" Mr. Worth's mouth twisted into a wry grimace. "After all, you are the more mature party."

Alexis's face hardened into an icy mask. This wasn't turning out at all the way she'd imagined.

"Sure, I'll be nice to Vanessa. Instead of telling her to shove her Greek cruise, I'll send her a politely worded refusal on the engraved stationery she sent me a month late for my birthday. You know, the box that still had the 'half price' sticker on the bottom." She gripped the arms of the fat leather chair as though she were holding on to a life raft.

It was Hugo Worth's job to pick up on people's moods, and Alexis certainly wasn't doing a good job hiding hers. But sometimes parental logic functions according to rules not discernible to a rational mind—or at least that's how it seemed to Alexis, based on what came out of her father's mouth next.

"Alexis, darling," he said in the clipped, cool voice he usually reserved for tabloid journalists. "I won't have you getting writer's cramp. You're going to call your mother right now and accept her invitation. Graciously, I might add. Otherwise, that nice new car you've been expecting for a graduation present next year is going to stay in the showroom, and you'll be off to college bumming rides." He turned and picked the phone up from the receiver. "I suggest you make the call now, while my offer still stands. It expires in exactly one hour. If you let the time limit run out, you'll still have to go to Greece, even if I have to take you there myself."

Alexis struggled to hold back her tears as she reached for the phone. "Fine, I'll make the call. But not because of your lousy bribe. Material concerns no longer have a hold on my heart. I've made a sacred vow to live in the moment, even if that means yielding to a cruel and horrible fate. I hope you're happy."

Mr. Worth was somewhat puzzled. Since when had material concerns ceased to matter to Alexis? As far as he knew, her only mantra was "shop till you drop." Another one of her phases, he thought. We'll see if this one lasts until the next sample sale.

Meanwhile, Helene was doing battle with her mother in the kitchen, trying to convince her that Alexis simply *had* to accompany her to Paris. Otherwise, her entire summer vacation would be ruined.

"Mom, you don't understand. The only reason Dad wants me to visit is to put on some big act for his new movie-star wife. After the introductions are made, I'll be left home to sweep the ashes while the two of them go off to the ball."

Brenda Masterson smiled pityingly at her daughter. "If I know your father, he'll have hired a whole army of servants to sweep up the ashes. Really, Helene, I think he just wants to see you."

Helene snorted with derision. "Please. If he wanted to see me, he would have sent for me long before now. It's been over a year since our last fabulous reunion."

"Give your father a little credit, Helene. The two of

you used to be so close. It sounds to me like he was just flummoxed by how quickly you've grown up."

Helene pretended to pull her hair out by the roots. "Mom, I can't *believe* you're defending him!"

Ms. Masterson said, "I am the last person to 'defend' your father. Remember, I know his faults better than anyone. The fact remains, though, that he's your dad. And our custody arrangement says that you're to spend summer vacations with him."

"*Plus* holidays, *plus* alternating weekends. Whatever happened to those?"

"It's not easy, with him living in Europe."

"Give me a break, Mom! Daddy moved to Paris last year. He could have asked me to visit way before now. He chose not to." Big tears started spilling from her eyes, splashing onto the kitchen counter.

Ms. Masterson reached to smooth her daughter's hair. "Now, now, sweetheart, none of that. You're really making things out to be much worse than they are. Why not look at the bright side? Even if the visit goes badly, you'll still be in Paris. I would think a smart girl like you would jump at the chance to visit a city that's renowned for its art, music, and culture."

An hour ago, Helene had been thinking exactly the same thing. But without Alexis along, what had once seemed so inviting now seemed dull as dishwater, and she cried out, "What kind of geek do you think I am, Mom? Do you really think I want to spend the summer poking around museums and bookstalls? I'm seventeen years old. I want to have fun on my vacation. Go to a few parties? Maybe meet some boys?"

Helene's mother assumed a worried look. "Sweetheart, I thought you *liked* going to museums and bookstalls. I thought parties and boys were more along Alexis's line."

"Yeah, well, I'm *sick* of museums and bookstalls. I want some excitement for a change! You never see Alexis mooning around here Friday nights, waiting for the phone to ring."

"When's the last time *you* mooned around the house on a Friday night? You never stay home on the weekends! You're always off to some party or club meeting or retreat. You could hardly be called a wallflower."

With a guilty pang, Helene realized how little her mother knew about her dating history. She had hardly mentioned her first boyfriend, Jeremy, when they were going out (not that a loser like him was *worth* mentioning), and she had never even told her about Lazlo, preferring to keep their relationship a secret. Still, this was no time to confess that she didn't spend all her nights at the library.

Pretending to take an interest in her already ragged

manicure, Helene said, "Oh, all that is buddy-buddy type stuff. Going out bowling. Hanging out at the mall. Singing karaoke. I'm talking about boy-girl stuff. I can't remember the last time I had a date." Predictably, her face flushed. It always did when she told a lie. Helene remembered exactly when her last date was: August 28, when Lazlo took her to Hyde Park for a farewell picnic. They had kissed passionately in the late-summer sun, vowing to write each other every week.

Ms. Masterson looked at her daughter affectionately. "Sweetheart, don't be in such a hurry to grow up. You're just a late bloomer. Romantics like you usually are. I know I was. When I was seventeen, I read *Jane Eyre* until it fell apart in my hands. In between chapters, I prowled the halls of my high school, trying to find a boy to be *my* Mr. Rochester. Naturally, it was a fairly fruitless search."

Despite herself, Helene gave a gruff laugh. "I'll bet. So what are you saying, that real life has nothing to do with romance?"

Ms. Masterson shook her head. "I'm saying not to push yourself. Enjoy your youth. Romance will come to you; it just takes time. Until then, keep reading and dreaming. Then, someday when you least expect it, Prince Charming will come along and sweep you off your feet."

Prince Charming? Helene thought. Where did one

find a Prince Charming in a world where most marriages have the shelf life of a gallon of milk? Even Lazlo, who seemed pretty close to Prince Charming, had suddenly vanished from the face of the earth. Helene wasn't buying this line at all.

"Like Daddy swept you off your feet?" she asked. "That story certainly didn't have a happy ending."

Ms. Masterson turned red with rage. "Helene, I really can't have you talking to me like that. I raised you to be independent, not insolent. The fact remains, you're still seventeen years old, you're still my daughter, and you're *still* going to Paris. Without Alexis. Case closed!" she added loudly when Helene's mouth opened to protest. And, turning on her heel, Ms. Masterson marched out of the kitchen. Her footsteps were loud and angry.

As if on cue, Alexis walked in. "It went that well, huh?"

"Don't ask." In one perfectly synchronized motion, Helene yanked open the freezer door while Alexis rummaged around the kitchen drawer for two spoons. Minutes later, they were in a huddled conference over a pint of mocha almond fudge. Mocha almond fudge not being the most Zen-like of substances, the sisters had gone to Helene's room, where the walls were not painted white. The color of the walls was a bit of a mystery, in fact, as the room was completely covered by posters, pictures cut from magazines, strings of Christmas lights, and one big mirror encrusted with beads that Helene had glued on after watching an episode of *Trading Spaces*.

Helene pushed at pillows and clothes until there was enough space for her and Alexis. She flopped down on her stomach, while Alexis settled herself in her yogic posture.

"Ugh," Helene said, stabbing at the ice cream. "Mom thinks visiting Paris is an incredible learning opportunity I simply can*not* afford to miss."

Alexis shook her head when Helene proffered the pint to her. "I know. And Dad can't imagine why I'd want to go to a hot, stuffy city like Paris while I could be cruising around the Mediterranean with the Wicked Witch of the West."

"You should have seen the look on Mom's face when I told her that this summer I'm only interested in parties and boys."

Alexis burst out laughing. "You did not tell her that!"

"Basically. But I'm sick of being everyone's favorite nerdy bookworm."

Alexis smiled. "Well, you *are* a bookworm."

"Not funny," Helene grumbled.

"Yeah? Well, my dad thinks my sole aim in life is shopping and suntanning."

"Do you think they'll ever come to grips with the fact

that we're practically grown women?" Helene asked, spooning up the last of the ice cream.

"No. Until we're eighteen, we'll have to follow their stupid rules."

"Which means going our separate ways this summer. Gosh, I'm going to miss you, Lex."

"Fear not. Zen Master Lexy will be with you in spirit. In fact, I'm going to fix it so that you have the most romantic summer of your entire life. You won't have a chance to miss me, once I give you your assignment."

"Assignment? What assignment? I just told my mother I won't be doing anything remotely academic while I'm in Paris."

"Trust me, Helene, this assignment has nothing to do with literature, or history, or any of that other boring stuff you're always reading about. Although, if you pull it off, you'll be as famous as Marie Antoinette!"

"I'd be happy just to make a few friends," Helene said mildly.

"Don't underestimate yourself, Helene. If you follow my instructions, you'll be treated like royalty. By the end of the summer, you'll have the whole city eating out of your hand."

"Just so long as I don't offer them cake."

"Haven't you heard, sweetie? French women don't get fat! They'll take whatever you offer them, and love it!

And as far as French men are concerned . . ." Alexis began waltzing around the room with an imaginary partner, humming, "Some Day My Prince Will Come."

"Sounds like just the kind of mission I need." Helene laughed as her sister continued to dance around the room. "Come on and help me pack. . . . I need to leave in two days. It will take at least that long to get my bags packed."

Three

Mission: Impossible?

The girls were at Kennedy Airport, surrounded by a mound of luggage. Helene was decked out in a pink Chanel suit, thinking it was best to wear something French for her first trip to Paris. Being Helene, she had added a few distinctive touches: safety pin earrings, plus black nail polish, stacked rainbow wedge shoes, and Cleopatra eye makeup. Heads turned.

Alexis smiled indulgently at her sister. "Somehow, I don't think you'll have any trouble attracting attention in France." She was dressed in a crisp white linen dress and white sling-back sandals. White-framed sunglasses were pushed on top of her head, holding her straight dark hair away from the near-aristocratic angles of face.

"Speaking of attracting attention," Helene said, "it looks like you're about to make a couple of new converts." She nodded toward two teenage boys wearing backpacks and staring at them openly. The taller one had red hair, green eyes, and freckles. Incredibly, he was wearing a pair of overalls and a red flannel shirt. His friend had dirty blond hair and wore a checkered blue shirt that looked like his mom had ironed it. The boys couldn't take their eyes off the MasterWorth sisters.

Alexis slipped her sunglasses down to her nose. "Sorry, I'm afraid the new me can't be bothered to engage in any frivolous flirting." she said. "Besides, they're total geeks. Overalls? No thanks."

Helene laughed. "Paris won't be any fun without you, Zen Master Lexy," she said. "How am I ever going to compete with Margot Morganne? She's, like, the epitome of grace and sophistication."

"Helene, you shouldn't have to compete with Margot for your dad's affection. You're his daughter, she's his wife. Just be content with who you are, and the rest will take care of itself."

"Wise words indeed. Hey, Lexy, do me a favor. Remember your own advice when you're sailing around the Greek Isles with Vanessa the Vain. If she starts modeling a string bikini in front of the first mate, close your eyes and keep chanting. Remember, meditation and murder don't mix." Helene gave her a playful tug.

Alexis laughed. "I'll try to remember. Hey, why are we focusing on our stupid parents, anyway? We're both seventeen and free for the summer. Let's vow to make this one to remember, starting now. Which reminds me, I've got your assignment." She looked into her white designer shoulder bag and pulled out a manila envelope.

Helene reached for it eagerly. "Great. I've been dying to know how my transformation from a poor, neglected stepchild into a magnificent princess is supposed to come about."

Alexis held the envelope high over her head, just out of reach. "No dice, Cinderella. You're not to open this until after the plane takes off from New York. Transitions are best made while in transit." She put the envelope into Helene's waiting hands.

"So sayeth Lexy. Got it, chief. Anything else?"

"Nothing I can think of. Come on, let's get this luggage checked while there's still room on the plane." Helene leaned to grab the handle of the nearest suitcase, but Alexis held up a forbidding hand. "Princesses don't carry their own bags, dear." She beckoned to the two backpackers. The boys looked behind them to make sure that she was gesturing to them, then looked at each other before running to her.

"You need something?" the redhead asked. Up close, his freckles were even more pronounced.

"Who better to carry your luggage than a pair of big, strong country boys?" she whispered to Helene. To the guys, she said, "Oh, I just knew I could count on you to get us out of this jam. You see, my friend here was a little overzealous in her packing. Now she's got to check all these bags and she's under strict doctor's orders not to lift anything heavy. So we were just wondering . . ."

"If we could help carry your bags?" asked Red. "Sure, we'd be happy to."

The other boy eyed Alexis suspiciously. "Why don't you carry them? She's your friend."

Helene gave him a bright smile. "I'm sure you don't mean to be rude. This is obviously the first time you've been in the presence of a priestess. You see, my friend here, Zen Master Lexy, has renounced all earthly distractions. Carrying these bags would break her vows of spiritual purity."

"Meaning she's too lazy to help?" he asked.

Red gave his friend a poke. "Shut up, Tommy. We can hardly let a woman of Master Lexy's distinction go back on her vows. Say, do these vows happen to include celibacy, or are they just restricted to toting heavy objects around?"

Alexis smiled. "I cannot reveal the ancient secrets of my order. I do know, however, that the universe has a way of rewarding those who perform kind deeds for others." She gave one of her dazzling smiles.

Red turned as bright as his hair, then handed his friend two of the heaviest bags. He grabbed a zebra-striped cosmetic case, and the two of them staggered off to the baggage check, leaving the girls to say their good-byes.

Helene swept Alexis into a hug. "Well, I guess I'd better be going. Thanks for all the moral support."

Alexis squeezed her tightly. "Don't forget the envelope. And don't worry about Margot. Who knows? The two of you might even hit it off. Think positively and move gently."

"Okay, I'll envision the gentlest way possible of throwing her beneath the métro."

"I'll make a Buddhist of you yet," Alexis laughed.

Helene stretched out in first class. One thing was for sure: Her father wasn't a cheapskate. Judging from Margot Morganne's jewels, he wasn't skimping on his new wife, either. At the Toronto Film Festival, she had worn a sapphire necklace that matched the color of her eyes. At Cannes, she had been dripping with diamonds. When *Paris Match* asked Margot what her new husband thought about her love of expensive jewelry, she said, "Trevor tells me that I'm more precious than any of the stones in my jewel box."

Puke.

Idly, Helene wondered if it would be over the top to wear pearl earrings with a stainless-steel tongue stud to her first dinner in Paris. Oh, well, she'd figure it out

when she got there. In the meantime, there was Alexis's
envelope. Helene unsealed it just as the plane was taking
off. Inside was a photo of a stunning guy, which had been
ripped from a glossy magazine. The picture was accom-
panied by a dossier that Alexis must have mocked up on
the computer. It read:

Name: Daniel D'Artois, aka "the Prince of Paris"
Height: 6'1"
Hair: Thick and luscious
Eyes: Strictly bedroom
Home: Paris, France (duh)

Background: Son and heir of Alain D'Artois, owner and
head designer of Vedette, the hottest fashion house in
France.

Your Mission (Should You Choose to Accept It): Daniel
would be a jewel in any girl's crown. Use your womanly
wiles to capture his heart. This is an assignment of international importance! Relations between France and
America have never been colder. It's up to you to bridge
the gap.

Helene put down the dossier and frowned. It was easy
enough for cool, sophisticated Alexis to wrap the hottest

bachelor in France around her little finger. Guys took just one look at her and started frothing at the mouth. Helene's admirers had been different. Sure, they couldn't help but notice her wild style, but what really drew them was her great sense of humor and warm personality. These assets were fine for attracting a boy like Lazlo, but she suspected they wouldn't seem so compelling to the Prince of Paris. How on earth am I going to make a guy like Daniel D'Artois interested in me? Helene wondered, staring off into space.

A flight attendant came by with a glass of champagne, but when he saw that Helene was underage, he offered her a sparkling water instead. As she drank the water, twirling the straw with her fingers, she had a sudden revelation. Of course! she thought, suddenly figuring out how to accomplish her new mission. Her new stepmother was one of the biggest film stars in France. Margot could throw them together at some big social function, say at a fashion show or movie premiere. Although Daniel D'Artois might not fall in love with her at first sight, if she somehow wangled an introduction to him, she just might catch this prince before the end of summer. Of course, this plan would require being extra nice to Margot, but maybe Alexis was right. Maybe her haughty, snobbish looks were the product of makeup artists, hairstylists, and airbrushing. Maybe instead of being a wicked step-monster, she'd really be more of a fairy godmother.

Helene picked up Daniel's photo again. Curly dark hair, smoky gray eyes, chiseled nose. That nose. Her mind flashed back to Lazlo. He used to tilt his head just before he'd kiss her so that their noses wouldn't bump. She wondered if she'd have to tilt her head to kiss this Daniel D'Artois. After all, his nose was as straight as an arrow. The rest of him wasn't too bad either. For a split second, Helene felt guilt pricking her conscience. Then a wave of anger washed over her.

"Why should I feel guilty about thinking of another guy?" she muttered as she accepted a hot towel from the smiling flight attendant. "I haven't heard from him in weeks. For all I know, he's been dating some British bimbo while I've sat home alone, waiting for him to return my e-mails." She peered at the photo again. "All right, Mr. D'Artois. Get ready to be swept off your well-shod feet."

She tilted her seat back and pulled the blue airline blanket up to her neck. And what if Lazlo did resurface, armed with a very good excuse as to why he hadn't been returning her e-mails? she asked herself. Well, it wouldn't be so bad to have two boys fighting for her undying affection. In fact, it might be a very nice change. Smiling, she fell asleep.

Four

Fleurs du Mal

Back in Scarsdale, Alexis was packing for her Grecian cruise. She filled suitcase after suitcase with all the white swimsuits, sundresses, blouses, skirts, and shoes she'd acquired since becoming a Buddhist. (Admittedly, she'd felt a bit decadent when she'd emptied out her entire closet in order to refill it with all-white clothing. She consoled herself with the thought that the local Salvation Army was about to have its best season ever.) Contrary to what her family thought, though, this latest form of dress wasn't merely a fad. It was a means to solve some very serious problems.

According to Alexis's research, white was the favored color of Buddhists because it promoted clarity of purpose, and she desperately needed to get clear on a few issues. Ever since Christmas break, her emotions had been in tumult. This was a strange sensation for Alexis, who prided herself on her logic and detachment. Unlike Helene, she never panicked when faced with a difficult

situation. Instead, she examined the issue from every possible angle, then carefully constructed a plan to overcome
the obstacle at hand.

Last December, though, she had overheard a conversation between her dad and stepmom that made her
reconsider her entire direction in life. The whole family
had gone to Aspen for winter break, where Mr. Worth
had rented a luxurious cabin. The first night they were
there, Alexis and Helene stayed out until three a.m., par-
tying with a bunch of other kids who were also vacation-
ing in the area. If it had been a school night, their parents
would have gone crazy, issuing all sorts of punishments
and ultimatums. Because it was winter break, though,
they decided to cut the girls a little extra slack, and let
them go to bed without a lecture.

The next morning, Alexis got up early to go on a walk.
No matter how late she'd been up the night before, she
always woke at sunrise. Helene, on the other hand, made
a point of staying in bed for as long as she possibly could,
especially on holidays. Alexis didn't mind being by herself. She enjoyed walking along the freshly shoveled
paths alone, watching the sun turn the snowy landscape
into a carpet of diamonds.

She was taking off her boots in the living room when
she heard strained, hushed voices from her parents' bedroom. That was weird, since Mr. Worth and Ms.

Masterson hardly ever fought. Ever fearful of divorce, Alexis put her ear to the door and discovered they were arguing about her and Helene's late-night escapades.

"After all," Ms. Masterson was saying to Mr. Worth, "they're both going to college next year. It's not like we'll be able to impose a curfew on them then."

"Yeah," Mr. Worth grumbled. "But that doesn't stop me from worrying about them. I mean, Helene's got a good head on her shoulders. You don't have to worry about her running off with some tanned ski instructor. But Alexis—"

Ms. Masterson interrupted. "Alexis is fine! Her judgment is just as sound as Helene's."

Alexis's father sighed. "Yes, I'm not giving her enough credit. But you have to admit she takes after her mother, in certain ways."

Alexis pulled her ear away from the door, ran into the bathroom, and locked it. She sank to the floor and wrapped her arms around her knees, sobbing into a folded wash cloth. Is that what they really think of me? she wondered. Some mindless fortune hunter who's just shopping her way through life?

Eventually, Alexis managed to stop crying and took a shower. By the time she emerged from the bathroom, she was back to her cool, detached self. Nobody would ever know, looking at her as she emerged, that beneath her placid exterior raged a mass of insecurities. Unlike Helene, she almost never worried about her looks or what other people thought of her. Not only that, she considered herself to be extremely focused. She wasn't the type to take up knitting one week only to abandon a half-made sweater for judo lessons the next. When she set goals, she focused on them like a laser until they were completed.

So how come her own dad thought she was an empty-headed gold digger? Granted, he hadn't used those exact words, but the implication was there. *She takes after her mother.* Well, if that wasn't an insult, she didn't know what was. Alexis knew how much her father hated Vanessa. Even if she had her own problems with her mom, it still hurt to hear her being bad-mouthed. Truthfully, Alexis had missed her mother terribly since the divorce. Ms. Masterson was great, so far as step-mothers were concerned, but nobody could replace your real, live, flesh-and-blood mom. Even a mom who didn't seem to want you around.

After the divorce, when her father was granted full custody, Vanessa vanished into thin air. Every once in a while, Alexis got a call from some sun-drenched island, but those conversations were always brief and stilted. Inevitably, the connection would get so weak that one of them would have to hang up. Her father and Ms.

Masterson tried to reassure her that Vanessa really loved her, and that the only reason she didn't visit was that she was "a kind of gypsy" (her stepmother's words) who preferred "a vagabond lifestyle" (her father's, which he barely managed to say with a straight face). Alexis didn't buy it. She knew that if her mother really cared, she'd find a way to visit her, even if it meant staying in one place for a whole month or even two.

Maybe that was it, though. Maybe her father didn't think Alexis herself was capable of forming meaningful attachments to people. Admittedly, she *did* have quite a roster of boyfriends. Nobody in the family could keep track of them, they came and went so fast. It wasn't that she was fickle as much as she'd never developed strong feelings for any of her suitors, and she couldn't see any point in continuing a relationship if there wasn't any emotional depth to it.

Even last summer's fling with Simon was something of a disappointment. Sure, they'd had a fun time exploring London together, and he'd been a great kisser, but he never gave her that heavenly, floaty feeling that Helene obviously had when she was with Lazlo.

As she thought about these things during the days and weeks after they'd returned from winter vacation, a horrible thought began to gnaw at Alexis's mind. What if she was incapable of falling in love? The possibility frightened her. What she needed was a purpose in life, one that didn't involve any emotional attachments. Frankly, she didn't see much purpose in sailing around the world on an endless vacation, like her mother. Alexis wanted more for herself than that. But what?

She thought about women she admired. Oprah Winfrey, Martha Stewart, Coco Chanel. None of them were married, but they did have successful careers. The thought of having an all-consuming passion, one that precluded any messy relationships, appealed greatly to Alexis's logic. There was still one hitch, though: What kind of career should she pursue? The question dogged her all through winter and spring.

Alexis wanted a job in which she could be totally self-reliant. Something that allowed her to create her own little universe, where no one could shatter her confidence. The kind of job that set her apart from the crowd, and proved that she was doing more than just passing time, waiting for a rich husband to come along.

The more she thought, the more despondent Alexis became. She began to wish she were more like her sister, who took an interest in everything. She could picture Helene being equally happy as a rock star or a forensic pathologist. Knowing her, she would probably try both by the time she was forty—with great success, of course.

Then, two months ago, just as she was about to write

Dr. Phil for help, she saw the article on Zen in *Real Simple*. The concept of purifying her life greatly appealed to her. She downloaded some more information on Buddhism from the Internet, and even checked out a few books on the subject from the library. Much to Alexis's astonishment, she drew great comfort from the Buddha's teachings, and began integrating them into her life.

Even after Zen had taught her some valuable coping skills, she hadn't expected it to reveal her life's purpose. Miraculously, it had. Just as she started turning her bedroom into an all-white sanctuary, it hit her: She loved making things beautiful. Decorating rooms, making over girlfriends, putting together outfits. What about a career in design?

It would be something she could do on her own, it would draw on her talents, and, best of all, it would make her financially independent. Nobody could ever accuse her of being a gold-digging parasite if she had a successful business of her own.

She ran the idea past Helene, who greeted it with gratifying enthusiasm. "Lexy, that's perfect. I think you'd make a great designer. What kind do you want to be?"

"I'm not sure yet, but I think if I remain open to the universe's bounty, the opportunity will present itself."

Thinking back on the conversation, Alexis smiled

affectionately. Her parents might think she was a total airhead, but she could always depend on Helene for support. She wondered how she'd fare this summer, without her sister's praise and encouragement. It had felt good when Helene had asked her advice about Margot. Poor kid . . . she really was suffering from the ugly stepchild syndrome. Alexis hoped she would give Margot the benefit of the doubt instead of deciding to hate her before she even got off the plane. It was like the Buddha said: The end to suffering can only come through wisdom and compassion. Maybe her sister would stop suffering once she gave Margot a chance to prove herself.

Come to think of it, maybe Vanessa deserved a chance to prove herself too. After all, she *did* invite her to spend the summer together. Alexis was the only child Vanessa had. Now that she was getting older, she was probably ready to renounce her globe-trotting ways. Or at least rein them in a bit for the sake of her daughter.

Alexis caught sight of the white roses that were sitting on her dresser. They were starting to droop, and the petals had gone brown around the edges. She fingered them thoughtfully. I'm through living in the past, Alexis thought. It's time I took my own advice and started living in the moment. Surveying her luggage, she wondered if it would be too materialistic to take another bag, then ended up packing two more.

There was a knock at the door as she clicked her last suitcase shut. Turning around, Alexis saw her father. He had a serious look on his face.

"Oh, Daddy, I'm so glad you're here. I wanted to tell you not to worry while I'm in Greece. I think you're right; this is going to be a turning point for mother and me."

Mr. Worth looked down at the white shag carpet. "Alexis, honey, another fax just came for you." He held out a sheet of white paper.

Alexis took it with trembling hands. The message was brief: *Change of plans. Must postpone trip for another time. So sorry, all love—Vanessa.*

"Well, at least she stopped calling herself 'Mom,'" Alexis said, trying to laugh but failing. She caught sight of the quote she had taped to her mirror, back when she first took up Buddhism: "The end to suffering can only come through wisdom and compassion." What a joke! How could she ever have fallen for such nonsense? She had a vision of herself picking up the vase of roses and hurling it at the mirror, but settled for curling her hands into white-knuckled fists.

Mr. Worth said brokenly, "Alexis, darling, I'm just so sorry. Please, let me—"

"What, Daddy? Buy me a car? Give me a tennis bracelet? Lend me your platinum card? Just forget it. All I want is . . ." she began sobbing uncontrollably.

Mr. Worth looked up. "What, baby?"

"A ticket to Paris on the next plane. I'm spending the summer in France with the only relative who really cares about me—Helene."

Five

An American in Paris

Helene took a deep breath before emerging into the waiting area of Charles de Gaulle Airport. She looked left, then right, but didn't see a trace of her father. People kept streaming off the plane, running into the loving embraces of friends and family. Meanwhile, Helene just stood there, looking awkward and feeling stupid. Finally, a big, burly man with a shaved head and thick mustache stepped forward. He was wearing a plain dark uniform that strained to stay buttoned over his ample torso.

"Excuse me, mademoiselle. Are you Helene Masterson?"

Helene broke out in a nervous smile. "Yes, that's me."

The man inclined his head in a demi-bow. "My name is Pierre. I am to conduct you to your father's house. Let's collect your baggage and be on our way."

Helene couldn't help but feel disappointed. A little piece of her had hoped her father would meet her at the airport. "You'd think he would take the time out of his schedule for his only daughter," she muttered under her breath.

"I'm sorry, mademoiselle, is there something you wanted?" asked Pierre.

"Nope, just my bags. They're the ones with the zebra stripes on them," Helene said, gesturing to the mountain of luggage being spat out of the carousel.

Pierre paled slightly, then began piling her trunks onto a metal cart, talking to himself bitterly in French. Uh-oh, she thought, I don't want to be making enemies on my first day here. In fact, I think I'm going to need all the allies I can get. She started helping him with the luggage, but he waved her away gruffly. She tried another approach.

"Pierre," she said brightly, using her best good-girl voice, "you know my stepmother—Margot, I mean. What's she like?"

For a second, it was as if a dark cloud had passed over Pierre's eyes. He opened his mouth, then shut it again. Finally, after a painful silence, he said, "*Je suis désolé, mademoiselle*. I cannot understand your question. My English is very poor." He gave the cart a big heave, and they started toward the exit.

Helene's nerves began to mount. Pierre could barely understand her, and she couldn't understand him at all.

She had taken Spanish in school for the past three years, believing it would be much more useful. She'd never expected her father to move to Paris. And while it was true that Spanish was very handy in New York, Helene could see it was of little use here. Normally, she was able to blast through social formalities with her quick wit and outgoing personality, but she quickly saw that the language barrier put her at a distinct disadvantage in France.

After loading the bags into the trunk of a black limousine, Pierre opened the back door with a flourish. As Helene scrambled in, she caught sight of a worn paperback in the front seat of the car: *The Bridges of Madison County*. Helene did a double take: The book was in *English*. It was open to the middle and placed facedown on the passenger seat, as if the reader had been drawn into the story and just abandoned it at the last minute. Pierre opened the driver's side door and slid into the front seat. Helene stared at the back of his head. Obviously, he *could* speak English, at least well enough to read a book in the language. So why had he pretended not to understand her question about Margot? Loyalty to his employer? Maybe, but that didn't account for that funny look he got when she mentioned Margot's name.

What kind of woman was this Margot Morganne? Helene shivered. Like it or not, she was about to find out.

• • •

Her father's house seemed to take up a full city block. Helene had always grown up in posh surroundings, but she was very impressed by the majestic lemon-colored building that stood before her. Ornate, arched doorways; tall, gleaming windows; a graceful, columned balcony. It seemed like something out of a fairy tale. Seeing her zebra-striped luggage in the elegant hallway gave Helene a funny feeling. Back when he was married to her mother, they had lived in a funky Spanish bungalow in Westwood, an arty neighborhood in Los Angeles. She suspected this opulent home was more reflective of her stepmother's taste. How was her own style going to hold up in all this grandeur?

Her combat boots thudded heavily on the clean marble floor. Looking around the dimly lit hallway, she could see rich, ancient tapestries hanging from the wall, making the place feel like a dark cocoon for the rarest butterfly you could imagine.

"Helene? Is that you?" a deep voice called from the other end of the hall. She walked toward it.

"Yes, Daddy, I'm finally here." Her voice faltered in the darkness. Then her father came into view. Helene's eyes watered. He seemed so much older than when she had seen him last, not even two years ago.

"Daddy," she said in a choked voice, running into her

father's open arms. The two stood there for a moment, rocking back and forth. All the awkwardness of the Christmas debacle seemed to have vanished into thin air. Maybe he feels just as bad about that visit as I do, Helene thought. Well, if he's willing to forget the whole stupid episode, so am I.

Trevor Masterson broke away, as if embarrassed. "Helene, honey, I'd like you to meet my wife, Margot. Margot, my darling daughter, Helene." He gestured toward a small figure standing off to the side. A perfect mane of blond hair cascaded down the woman's back. She had big brown doe eyes and a mouth that made Angelina Jolie look like a Sunday school teacher. Her heart-shaped face even had a dimple in the chin.

My God, it's worse than I imagined, Helene thought as she moved forward to greet her. Of course, she recognized Margot from the many magazines that sported her image. Still, no photograph could convey how positively breathtaking she was. Standing next to her, Helene knew what Skipper must have felt when Barbie hit puberty.

Forcing a smile, she extended a hand to her step-mother, who looked as though she were being offered a rotting fish. Finally, she lifted her own hand and limply grasped Helene's for a brief second, then dropped it.

Helene stepped back, hurt by the utter lack of

warmth. Clearly, this woman did not relish the prospect of being her stepmother. Margot's huge eyes traveled slowly from Helene's tangled hair to her combat boots. Her disdain was obvious. Helene had never felt so self-conscious in her life. It was all she could do not to cower like a chastised puppy.

Evidently, her father didn't notice the tension between them, because he said, "I know you two are going to become fast friends. Helene, I think you'll find that it's almost impossible not to love Margot. She's got a naturally upbeat personality." He slipped his arm through Margot's.

Wow, her enthusiasm is blowing me away, Helene thought.

"Well, Helene, you must be very tired from your long trip. Why don't I show you to your room? Would you like something to eat?"

Helene's eyes flicked over to Margot's gorgeous figure. "No thanks," she lied. "I ate on the plane." Just then, her stomach gave a huge growl. Margot smirked.

Mr. Masterson looked blissful. "Well, I've arranged a big family dinner for us at seven," he said. "Why don't you get settled and we'll all meet in the dining room then." He moved his arm to Margot's shoulders, embracing her. She gave Helene a superior smile.

"Okay, Dad. I'll need a few hours to unpack, anyway."

Helene tried to match her father's upbeat tone, but to her ears she sounded like a cheerleader gone insane.

Turning to Helene, Margot said, "You Americans are famous for your healthy appetites. Therefore, I asked the chef to prepare a classic French menu. Onion soup, bacon salad, filet mignon au sauce béarnaise, new potatoes, and tarte tatin."

Helene's heart lifted at this apparent gesture of courtesy, only to have it plummet just as quickly when Margot continued, "Unfortunately, I will not be able to join in the feast. You see, I have a very important part coming up, and I must lose all this—how you say—baby fat." Margot pinched her waist, managing to grasp a millimeter of skin. Helene rolled her eyes.

Mr. Masterson said, "Margot here has just landed a terrific part in a movie. She plays an ... er ... a ... how exactly would you describe your character, darling?"

Margot said, "She is ... *comment dit-on? Oui,* a streetwalker."

"Must be quite a stretch for you," Helene said, trying hard to keep the sarcasm out of her voice.

Fortunately, Mr. Masterson seemed not to hear. He only had eyes for Margot. Giving his wife an affectionate squeeze, he said, "Yes, Margot's a wonder. Last year she was up for Best Actress at Cannes. And the film this year is a shoo-in for the Palme d'or, if not the Grand Prix. We'll all be attending the premiere together on Friday."

Margot snuggled into the crook of her husband's arm, looking like a spoiled cat.

Helene's heart sank. It was obvious that her father was head over heels in love with Margot. In fact, he adored her so much, he couldn't seem to conceive that someone *wouldn't* like her. If Helene complained that Margot was treating her poorly, no doubt he'd stick up for his wife, accusing her of petty jealousy. Well, maybe she *was* jealous of this stunning woman, but that didn't erase the fact that her stepmother was abominably rude.

If only Alexis were here. Helene always drew confidence from her beautiful, self-assured friend. Instead of taking Paris by storm together, though, she knew they would be begging for scraps of attention from their respective families all summer. How weird to feel orphaned when you had five parents between you.

Dinner at Chez Masterson was a quiet, creepy affair. Helene's dad sat at one end of the formal, polished table, Margot sat at the other. Helene was placed on the side, halfway between the two. Her halfhearted attempts at conversation were met with absentminded responses from her father, who was busy staring adoringly at Margot. Margot meanwhile was staring adoringly at her own reflection, courtesy of the mirror that was positioned just over Mr. Masterson's left shoulder.

Even though she had vowed to eat only a salad, Helene couldn't stop herself from loading her plate from every dish that was offered. After her long trip, the hot, fragrant soup seemed like just the thing to reinvigorate her. The filet mignon was even more appetizing, with the consistency of butter. Best of all were the crusty rolls, which literally melted in her mouth. Helene had to force herself not to reach for a third. Margot, on the other hand, turned her nose up at everything, confining her meal to cup after cup of black coffee, interspersed with a series of cigarettes.

"Please eat, darling," Mr. Masterson pleaded.

"I had a disgustingly big lunch," she said from behind a cloud of thick smoke. "Perhaps I will have something before I retire."

"It wouldn't hurt you to have some soup, or at least a bit of salad." Mr. Masterson's voice was deep with concern.

Margot gave an impatient shake of her head. "I prefer to eat small amounts throughout the course of the day. You Americans have a totally different attitude toward eating. Such big portions. No wonder you are all so big and strong. Even your women are tremendous, like giant oak trees."

Helene put her knife and fork down and tried sitting on her hands. Never in her life had she tasted anything as delicious. Normally, she would have no problem digging into a meal like this, even asking for seconds, but with Margot at her elbow, she felt like a blimp.

Use your mouth for something other than eating, she told herself, then turned toward her stepmother. Remember, this is the woman who could introduce you to Daniel D'Artois. Be nice to her.

"It must be really exciting to be an actress. Sort of like living somebody else's life for weeks at a time. Then, when you get bored with one life, you move on to another."

Margot shrugged. "For some, acting is an exciting challenge. For me, it comes so naturally and easily that it is sometimes . . . almost boring."

Helene frowned. "Then why do you do it?"

She shrugged again. This seemed to be her trademark gesture. "What else is there to do?" she asked, stubbing her cigarette out in a crystal ashtray, then motioning the butler for more coffee.

Despite herself, Helene's natural enthusiasm for life came bubbling to the surface. "Do? Why, there's lots of stuff to do when you don't have to work. You could paint, or draw, or write, or go back to school. I would think a beautiful woman like you would have tons of interests."

For a split second, Margot's poise faltered. Her

frightened expression was so fleeting that Helene couldn't be absolutely sure she had witnessed it. Her stepmother looked momentarily as though her deepest fear had been exposed. Then, just as quickly as the mask had begun to melt, it froze solid again.

Margot gave a chilly smile and said, "I'm afraid such activities would be just another source of boredom for me. You Americans lead such sheltered lives. It is part of your charm. But for a French woman such as myself, the prospect of sketching bowls of fruit seems very dull."

Mr. Masterson looked at his wife adoringly. "You see, Helene, acting is really just a diversion for Margot. Don't be fooled by her beauty. Beneath that gorgeous face, she really is a very deep person."

Yeah, if you call a rain puddle in the Sahara deep, Helene thought.

Just then, the butler came in. "Telephone for Mademoiselle Helene," he said, placing the instrument at her elbow.

"Who is it?" she asked excitedly. She would have welcomed a telemarketer at that point. When it turned out to be Alexis, her joy was palpable. "Lexy? Where are you?" She yelled into the phone, making Margot flinch. Helene jammed her finger into her free ear, even though it wasn't necessary. The only sound in the room was the wax dripping off the candles.

"You're kidding me! Oh, my God, that is the best!" Helene jumped out of her chair, sending her linen napkin fluttering to the ground. "What time is your flight getting in? Of course, you can stay here. No I haven't begun my assignment yet . . . ," she trailed off, conscious of her dining companions. She bent to retrieve her napkin, and as she did, hissed, "I can't discuss it now. We'll talk when you get here." Helene straightened up. "Yes, yes, I've got it. See you soon, sweetie! Bye."

For the first time since Helene arrived, Margot looked interested. "Who was that? Your boyfriend?"

The prospect of a young man staying under the same roof as his new wife clearly didn't sit well with Mr. Masterson. He leaned forward and said, "Now, just wait a minute, Helene. I don't think your mother would approve."

Helene's laugh boomed out. "No Daddy, that wasn't my boyfriend. It was Alexis. She's coming to stay with us this summer. I invited her before, figuring that the last thing a couple of newlyweds would want was a teenager moping around the house all the time." There, Helene thought. He can hardly argue with that logic. I mean, the guy barely even notices I'm in the room when Margot's around.

Surprisingly, Mr. Masterson hesitated. "Well, I don't know. I thought it would be nice for us to enjoy some family time this summer."

Margot jumped in. "Trevor, this is perfect. Now that I am between films, we can have a second honeymoon, of sorts. I'm sure Helene will have lots more fun in Paris with someone her own age."

Helene could barely suppress a laugh. "Someone her own age." Margot was only eight years older than she was. Still, if her stepmother was going to make a case for Alexis's visit, Helene was hardly going to stop her.

"Besides, Daddy, she's already on her way. I know it's short notice, but she had a last-minute change of plans. She was going to visit her mom this summer, but Vanessa cancelled . . . again. I think she could use a friend right now. You know, it's not easy being a child of divorce." Helene let her eyes fill with tears. Margot gave her a shrewd look. That's right, honey, Helene thought to herself. You're not the only one in this family who can act.

Heaving a sigh, Mr. Masterson said, "I wish you would have asked before inviting Alexis over. Still, under the circumstances, I guess it's the least we can do for the poor girl. Imagine, having to spend a whole summer away from family."

"Heaven forbid," Helene murmured.

Mr. Masterson beamed at his daughter, while Margot looked disgusted. The butler returned.

"Would mademoiselle care for dessert?" he asked after he had removed Helene's dinner plate.

She threw back her shoulders and looked Margot square in the eye. "Sure, why not?" Nobody was going to stand between her and a big piece of tarte tatin. Now that Alexis was coming, she was ready for a double helping of fun.

Six

Dangerous Liaisons

"Zen Master Lexy!" Helene sang out across the crowded gate. "Welcome to the City of Light."

She ran to hug her stepsister as if they'd been separated for years, when it had in fact been a little over twenty-four hours. Alexis was clad from head to toe in red. She wore a red camisole, red capri pants, red sandals, and a red purse. She gave Helene a brief, hard hug.

"No more Buddhism," she said. "I've officially returned to my old, self-obsessed ways. After getting Vanessa's latest note, I realized that, in my case, unconditional love is really double-speak for me being a door-mat."

Helene nodded sympathetically. "I know what you mean. I came here trying to give Margot the benefit of the doubt, and guess what? She's nastier than I thought. In fact, she makes Vanessa sound positively saintly."

"Actually, I'm beginning to think Vanessa's approach to life is right on target," Alexis said, tossing her long, dark hair over her shoulder. "Find a rich husband, get a divorce, collect a huge alimony, and live happily ever after."

Wrapping her arm around her sister's shoulder, Helene said, "Come on, Lexy, you don't really mean that."

"Oh, don't I?" Alexis said. Her eyes sparkled like a cobra ready to strike. "Just watch me."

Helene knew better than to argue with Alexis when she was in this sort of mood. Changing the subject, she said, "Well, I'm glad you're here. It's nice to have someone around I can trust." She looked over her shoulder cautiously. "Hey, watch out for Pierre. He's Daddy's chauffeur. He pretends not to know English, but I think he's fluent."

Alexis stepped forward and gestured to Pierre. *"Vous êtes le chauffeur de Monsieur Masterson?"* she asked in a crisp, businesslike tone.

Pierre snapped to attention and practically clicked his heels. *"Oui, mademoiselle."*

She proceeded to give what Helene assumed were long, complicated instructions for handling her baggage. Pierre broke into a smile. A twinge of jealousy plucked at Helene's stomach. She never realized how good Alexis's French was. Throughout all their years in school together, Helene was considered the brain, while Alexis was

admired as the beauty. Hearing her stepsister's easy ban-
ter with Pierre, she felt decidedly stupid. *What are they
saying?* Helene wondered. She saw Alexis and Pierre
turn to look at her simultaneously. *Could they be talking
about me?*

"Helene, hurry up," Alexis called. "I can't wait to see
your dad's place. Pierre tells me that it's in the middle of
St-Germain-des-Prés. Are the shops to die for, or what?"

"Lexy, relax." Helene laughed. "I only got here yester-
day. And as soon as I heard you were coming, I decided
to wait till you got here to go exploring." As she spoke,
she felt a twinge of annoyance. Although her sister didn't
know a thing about France's history, she had obviously
made it her business to know the most fashionable places
to live, eat, and shop there.

Alexis threw up her hands in disgust. "Helene! You've
only got eight weeks to"—her eyes slid over to Pierre, and
her voice dropped—"attain your objective. There's not a
moment to lose!" She turned to issue more rapid com-
mands to Pierre, who ran off in the direction of baggage
claim.

"Well, I *was* planning to set off on my mission today,
but I decided instead to pick up my stepsister at the airport. . . ."

Alexis didn't seem to be listening. By now, they had
caught up to Pierre, and she began counting her suitcases.

Unlike Helene's luggage, Alexis's bags were handsome, understated, and classic. Zebra stripes versus light brown leather; ripped fishnets versus silk stockings. That was the difference between Helene and Alexis in a nutshell. Usually, the combination worked well. Guys who were interested in Helene thought Alexis was pretty but too uptight; boys who were attracted to Alexis thought her stepsister was cute but too free-spirited. Helene was beginning to wonder how things would translate now that they were in Paris.

Finally the bags were collected and they were in the limo zipping toward Chez Masterson. Alexis shook her head sympathetically as Helene told Alexis about dinner with her parents, then Helene huffed and puffed with anger when Alexis told her about Vanessa's last-minute cancellation. Confiding their troubles to each other rekindled the closeness between them, and by the time they pulled up to Trevor Masterson's house, the MasterWorth sisters felt ready to conquer all of France.

Helene dragged Alexis by the hand into the hall. The girls were laughing excitedly, giddy with the pleasure of being in Paris together. Helene pointed out the furniture, paintings, and tapestries, enjoying her stepsister's gasps of admiration. Then, as they were just entering the salon, Margot stepped into view. She looked more breathtakingly beautiful than ever, wearing a formfitting dress that showed off her magnificent figure to its best advantage. An antique gold necklace accentuated the delicate lines of her throat, and just a trace of makeup enhanced her golden complexion. She looked questioningly at Alexis, then Helene.

"Um, Margot, this is my best friend, Alexis Worth. She'll be staying with us this summer. Alexis, this is my father's new wife, Margot Morganne."

"Best friend? But I thought you were sisters." Margot's gaze was appraising. Clearly, she thought there was little resemblance between the two.

"We're best friends *and* sisters. Stepsisters, to be exact," Helene said.

Alexis extended a manicured hand. *"Enchantée de faire votre connaissance, Madame."* Again, the flawless accent. Margot was visibly impressed.

"I take it you have seen my movies in the States?"

Alexis gave a chilly smile. "No, actually, I think movies are a bore," Alexis lied. "I'd much rather go to the theater. That's where you can see *real* acting."

Eager to see her stepmother fly into a rage, Helene was astonished when Margot assumed an expression of total devotion toward Alexis.

"Well, perhaps you will have the chance to see some of them while you are in Paris. And even change your opinion of film acting?" Margot suggested.

"Perhaps," Alexis answered.

"Either way, it is a pleasure to meet you. I notice you have a wonderful fashion sense," Margot said, taking note of Alexis's all-red outfit.

"Yes, well, I plan to be a designer when I graduate college," Alexis said loftily.

"Your style is impeccable. I was beginning to wonder if American girls even possessed such a thing," Margot pronounced.

Helene stepped forward, trying to suppress the impulse to rip every hair from Margot's head. Before she got very far, she caught sight of Alexis from the corner of her eye. She shook her head almost imperceptibly. Helene stopped in her tracks and bit her tongue.

"Helene, I'd like to shower after that long plane ride. Afterward we can go out and explore the city." Alexis sounded cool and calm, like a maître d' issuing instructions in an expensive restaurant.

Helene went to show Alexis her room, which was right next to her own. Alexis followed with a light step, then softly closed the door that her sister was about to slam.

"Don't you see what a witch she is?!" Helene exclaimed as Alexis wrapped her in a soothing embrace.

"Yeah, she *is* pretty ghastly, all right. But I've got a

total read on her. Margot's the type who can only respect people who treat her with total indifference. Try to be her friend, and she'll laugh in your face. Ignore her, and she'll totally kiss up to you."

"How sad." Helene sank down on the bed. "Why do you think she acts that way?"

Alexis shrugged. "Low self-esteem. You know the saying: I wouldn't want to belong to any club that had me for a member."

"So ignore her and I'll have her eating out of my hand, right?"

Alexis looked at her sister and sadly shook her head. "No, hon, I don't think Margot will ever eat out of your hand. For one thing, you'll always pose a threat, as far as your dad is concerned. Secondly, you're way too nice to treat anybody like dirt for long."

Helene grinned. "Unlike you, huh? You certainly gave her the cold shoulder out there. Worked like a charm too."

"It must be my mother's genes," Alexis said in a flat voice. "I have a feeling I'm going to like this city." Alexis crossed to examine the elaborate bathroom, which was decked out with gold fixtures and floor-to-ceiling mirrors. Endless Alexises were reflected throughout the marbled room. She ran to the tub and opened the taps all the way. The plumbing hidden in the walls was every bit as old world as the faucet: Only a trickle spilled from the gold faucet and splashed into the tub. The hidden pipes creaked loudly.

"Paris isn't *all* elegance and sophistication, you know," Helene shouted over the noise. Alexis thought she meant the plumbing, at first, but her sister went on to say: "This city has a pretty violent history. Remember the statue of Jean-Paul Marat we saw in London, when we visited Madame Tussaud's Wax Museum?"

"Nuh-uh," Alexis yelled. "Which one was that?"

"You know, the guy who was stabbed in the neck while taking a bath? He was a revolutionary who advocated violence, only to be viciously killed himself." Helene's voice was cheerful, as it always was when recounting some historical tidbit.

Alexis stepped into the tub. "Hey, don't be using me as target practice for Margot. I just got here!"

"Well, like I told you, I've really only seen the airport and this house," said Helene.

"Never fear, my darling sister," said Alexis, settling herself in the two inches steaming water that had managed to flow from the faucet. "Once I get cleaned up—if it's even possible to get cleaned up with plumbing this bad—we'll do some reconnaissance. Remember, I gave you a mission, and I fully expect you to carry it out."

• • •

That night at dinner, the girls recounted their afternoon to Mr. Masterson. They had gone shopping on the Rue du Four, pigged-out on *moules frites* at the Café de la Mairie, and flirted with boys on the steps of the art school.

For once, Mr. Masterson wasn't totally wrapped up in Margot. He seemed to be enjoying the girls' stories, laughing and asking questions. Finally, after a particularly hilarious account of Helene's first encounter with a bidet, Margot broke in.

"I hate to interrupt such a happy scene, but I have some exciting news."

Alexis and Helene exchanged glances. The Ice Queen? Excited?

Mr. Masterson leaned forward. "Darling, don't keep us in suspense. Come out with it."

"I was getting fitted for my gown at Vedette, when I ran into Alain D'Artois. Such a sweet man. Always makes a point to greet me personally whenever I arrive at his show room. He mentioned he was beginning a summer internship for students interested in fashion design. When I told him about our young friend here, and her hopes of becoming a designer?" Margot inclined her wineglass toward Alexis. "He graciously invited her to join the team for the summer."

Alexis's face lit up. "You mean I'd be learning fashion

design at the world's most prestigious couture house! I can't believe it!"

Margot laughed and said, "Not learning, developing your talent. I should have never suggested you for the job if I thought you had no aptitude for fashion."

"Hey, what about me?" Helene asked.

Margot shook her head sadly. "I am sorry, Helene. Alain is a very good friend to me, and I could hardly recommend you for a job that is beyond your skills."

Seeing his daughter's distress, Mr. Masterson tried to come to the rescue. "Besides, honey, this is your vacation. You're not really interested in going to a dingy little office when you could be out enjoying Paris?"

"And just how am I supposed to enjoy Paris when my best friend is toiling away in a dingy little office?" Helene demanded.

Margot gave a saccharine smile. "Why, I imagine a girl with all of your curiosity can think of countless things to do with your time. Painting, reading, drawing . . ."

Helene flushed, furious with Margot. Turning to her friend, she noticed a dreamy, faraway expression on her sister's face. Oh no, Lexy, Helene thought. Not you, too!

But apparently the prospect of a job with Vedette was too tempting for even Alexis to resist. She was already envisioning a new fabric pattern based on the antique wallpaper that hung in her bedroom. "An internship at

Vedette!" she breathed. "Oh, Madame Masterson, how can I ever thank you?"

Margot patted Alexis's hand and said, "Please, call me Margot. All my good friends do."

Helene jumped up from the table. "May I be excused? I'm feeling a little sick." She fled the room.

A few minutes later, Alexis followed. "Helene, I'm sorry. It's just that this is a chance of a lifetime. I've always been interested in fashion design. With this internship, I can get a job anywhere I want. You must see that."

"And what about our summer in Paris?" Helene choked out. "I thought we were going to spend all our time together. What's wrong with me? I feel like I have the plague. First Lazlo stops writing. Then I find out my new stepmother thinks I'm not only ugly but dull, too. And now my best friend is leaving me out in the cold."

"Helene, I'm not leaving you out in the cold. I'm simply taking a job of a lifetime!"

"From your new best friend, Margot Morganne. I don't know why I should be surprised you two get along so well."

As soon as she said the words, Helene wished she could take them back. But from the look on Alexis's face, she knew it was too late.

"And what is that supposed to mean? Since I got here, all you can talk about is your evil stepmother and how she's always stealing your father's attention. My mother tosses me aside like a used-up Kleenex and you don't even ask how I'm feeling! And now you want to make me feel guilty when something good finally happens to me."

Helene felt as though she had been kicked in the stomach. Usually, when one of them started yelling, the other would crack a joke or make a face and they would both start laughing. This time, they could barely look at each other.

After a strained silence, Alexis turned on her heel and left the room.

Seven

Vive la Différence

That Monday, Alexis began her internship at Vedette. Normally, the prospect of starting such an exciting job would fill her with nervous anticipation, but the only feeling she could muster that morning was relief. She had no intention of speaking to Helene until her sister apologized. Until then, she planned to spend as little time at Chez Masterson as possible.

She woke early and slipped on a crisp linen suit. The seductive smell of fresh-brewed coffee beckoned her to the kitchen, which was agleam with stainless-steel appliances. A large plate heaped with fresh croissants was standing next to the percolator, with a note that read "Bon Appétit." Part of her was glad that she didn't have to make small talk over a formal meal, but another part of her was distressed that she'd be venturing out to her new job without the usual pep talk she'd get from her family. Fortunately, Helene's father had left detailed instructions for getting to Vedette by métro. He had wanted her to use the chauffeur, but she had insisted on getting to work the way all Parisians did—public transportation.

She was excited to read that Vedette was located on the rue du Faubourg-St-Honoré. Extensive reading of *French Vogue* had taught her that all the big couture houses were clustered along this street, which was on the Right Bank of the city. Alexis wondered, as she sipped her coffee idly, whether it would be considered treason-ous to shop at the other boutiques on her lunch hour. Well, she decided, she'd feel out the other interns when she got there.

Glancing at the clock, she realized that she had to leave now if she was going to get to work on time. She had a sneaking suspicion there was no such thing as being fashionably late, even in the world of haute couture.

Fortunately, the métro was surprisingly easy to navi-gate, especially compared to the New York City subway system. There's a lot to be said for public transit, thought Alexis, as she took a seat next to a handsome man in a stylish pinstriped suit. The car was crowded with com-muters, and her head filled with pride when she realized that she, too, was part of this bustling, busy mass on her way to work.

She transferred at Châtelet Station from the 4 to the 1 train with success, then got off at the Champs-Elysées. As she drew nearer to Vedette, it seemed that her heart began to pound in time to her brisk high-heeled footsteps. At last she stood before an elegant glass structure that shone in the early morning sun. Taking a deep breath, she pushed her way through the revolving door and into the sleek lobby.

Summoning all her courage, she approached the raven-haired receptionist, who looked like she should be modeling the new Vedette line instead of sitting behind its reception desk. "My name is Alexis Worth. I'm one of the summer interns," she said nervously. "Could you please direct me to the design studio?"

The receptionist consulted her clipboard, which contained a long list of names. Finding hers, she made a sharp tick next to it, before looking up. "Walk down this corridor, make the first left, then take the stairs down to the basement."

Alexis did a double take. Maybe her French wasn't as good as she'd thought. "Excuse me, did you say the *basement*?" she asked. The receptionist gave a chilly nod, then motioned her to step aside. Realizing that a long line was forming behind her, Alexis hurried down the hall, turned left, and saw a heavy metal door marked *Escalier*. Heaving it open, she saw a narrow iron spiral staircase, the kind that never failed to make her dizzy. She clutched the rail and began making her way down to the basement. Her high heels clacked noisily on the metal treads, and her narrow skirt made it difficult to navigate the corkscrew turns.

After what seemed like ages, Alexis reached the bottom of the staircase, which was located smack in the middle of an expansive, open-loft space. Drafting tables were scattered around the perimeter, and the cement floor was littered with glittering pins, snarls of thread, and scraps of fabric. A battered radio was blaring pop music from the left corner, and a row of dress mannequins stood in the right.

Young people ran in every direction, shouting to be heard over the din. The noise from the radio was bad enough, but was further compounded by the steady drone of sewing machines and the shrill ringing of telephones. For a minute, Alexis felt as though she'd fallen down a rabbit hole into a Wonderland even weirder than the one Alice had discovered. Off to one side a few people stood around gaping at all the activity. They must be new, like me, Alexis thought.

She began making her way in that direction when she caught sight of a tall young man leaning against one of the draft tables. He wore a crisp white shirt that was open at the collar, setting off his tanned skin to perfection. A tight pair of blue jeans revealed the sort of lean, muscular frame that never failed to excite Alexis's imagination.

Unfortunately, his dark head was bent over a copy of *Paris Match,* which he was flipping through with an impatient air. If only I could get a look at his face, Alexis thought impatiently.

Sensing he was being stared at, the man lifted his head and looked directly into her eyes. Alexis felt her knees buckle. He's absolutely gorgeous! She pretended to search for something in her purse, then sneaked a second look. God, he looks familiar, she thought. Then it hit her: He must be a model. Of course. She had probably seen his picture in a magazine somewhere. He'd probably been hired for a photo shoot and was waiting to go out on an assignment.

The man set aside his magazine and began moving toward her. It's a good thing I gave up all that Zen nonsense, thought Alexis. She tried relaxing her posture, and nearly toppled backward with the effort. It wasn't so easy to stand casually in three-inch heels. Struggling to retain her balance, she nearly fainted when the man brushed past her and stood on the lowest step of the staircase. He turned to address the room.

Cupping his mouth with his hands to form a megaphone, he yelled, "Welcome, everybody. Could we please have some silence?" The chattering stopped, and the sewing machines ground to a halt. A young man scuttled across the room to turn off the radio. The phones kept shrilling, but nobody moved to answer them. He smiled and said, "As you old-timers may have noticed, we've added some new faces to the crowd. For those of you who don't know me, I'm Daniel D'Artois, and I'll be in charge of the summer interns this year." He paused to smile at an open-mouthed Alexis as he said, "I look forward to working very closely with you all."

While Alexis was getting her feet wet at Vedette, Helene explored the city on her own. Despite her sadness that Alexis had abandoned her, she had to admit it was exhilarating. When she was with Alexis, she normally went from store to store, trying on shoes, jewelry, and clothes. It was fun enough, but Alexis never enjoyed the places Helene liked to shop, and vice versa. The day before, when they were still on speaking terms, they had spent almost as much time arguing over where to go next as they did in actual stores. Today, however, Helene was able to set the schedule according to her own tastes. And she found it marvelous.

First she went to have breakfast at a little outdoor café on the Rue Bonaparte. Even though Paris was a huge metropolis, the streets were lined with trees, and Helene enjoyed listening to the chirping of birds as she sipped her coffee and ate her croissant. She wanted to buy a newspaper, but there weren't any English-language ones in the little stall she spied across the street, so she contented herself with sitting back and watching the crowd go by.

One thing that surprised her was how well she fit in with other Parisians. Unlike people in the States, everybody seemed to have their own unique style. Men weren't afraid to wear colors like pink and purple, and even seemed secure wearing shirts with floral patterns. Plus, they smelled gorgeous. For some reason that Helene couldn't fathom, the American guys she knew never wore cologne. French men did, though, and she felt a little depraved when she paused to inhale each time her cute waiter strolled by.

The women were even more eye-catching than the men, clad in daring colors and bold patterns. The scene reminded her a little of New York, but there, "black" was the rule. Everyone dressed very sleek, not so much understated as refined. Here, accessories seemed to be a big deal: artfully tied scarves, fancy sunglasses, oddly shaped purses. Teenage girls seemed to enjoy experimenting with their hair color just as much as Helene did. She even saw a girl with a totally shaved head.

Despite all this, Helene still stuck out in a good way. Boys winked when they walked past; men touched their hands to their foreheads in mock salute. A young mother paused to admire her paisley leggings, and a school girl asked in broken English where she got her hair done. For

the first time, Helene felt as though her style was working in her favor.

Later, she had fun strolling through the Luxembourg
Garden and pausing to admire all the gorgeous roses that
were just coming into bloom. If Alexis were here, she'd
be nagging her to duck into some expensive boutique.
Now that Helene was going solo, she could literally stop
and smell the roses.

Another thing Helene loved about Paris was the dogs.
(Alexis was a cat person.) They came in all shapes and
sizes, and everybody seemed to have one. Granted, the
lack of pooper-scooper laws was a drag—Helene had had
a few narrow escapes on the crowded sidewalks—but it
was fun pausing to greet squatty little dachshunds, regal-
looking poodles, and mischievous mutts. The language
barrier didn't seem to be a problem when you fussed over
someone's pet.

"I must have been crazy to think I couldn't have a
good time in Paris without Alexis," Helene muttered as
she pretended not to hear a boy's admiring whistle. It was
positively liberating to do what you wanted, when you
wanted, in a city this glorious. She ducked into a book-
shop and was delighted to find a whole selection of nov-
els written in English. She was startled to realize that two
hours had passed when she next looked at her watch.

Walking out into the late afternoon sunshine, she

sauntered past a row of shops. Suddenly, she stopped short in front of a boutique window. It held the most delicious tangerine-colored dress. I could wear it to Margot's premiere! she thought, and raced inside the store to examine it.

Sensing an eager customer, the proprietress, a middle-aged woman sporting a bottle green pantsuit with velvet lapels, glided forward. "Can I help you with something, *chérie?*" she asked in heavily accented English.

Her face fell. "How did you know I was American?" she asked.

The proprietress nodded at the English-language book beneath Helene's arm: *A Farewell to Arms*. "I hope I have not offended you?" she asked. "Actually, I adore Americans."

Helene flushed happily. "No, you haven't offended me. I had just begun to think that, here in Paris, I almost blended in."

The proprietress had a cozy, bubbling laugh that put Helene even more at ease. "Somehow I doubt you'd blend in anywhere, my dear. You have a style all your own."

If a shopkeeper had said that to Helene back at home, she'd take such a comment as a polite put-down. Here, in Paris, she knew it was a compliment. "Thanks. That's the nicest thing anybody's said to me in a long time."

The woman's tone became businesslike. "And what can I do for you?"

"Well, I'm going to a movie premiere on Friday night. I wasn't really looking forward to going, but when I passed by your window and saw this dress, I suddenly got excited."

The shop owner nodded judiciously. "Yes, it will bring out your green eyes beautifully. Of course, you'll want some green jewelry with it, to add more visual interest."

Helene nodded eagerly. "That's just what I was thinking. Do you have anything in mind?"

"Right this way, Mademoiselle," said the proprietress, leading her to a large glass case filled with all sorts of gorgeous necklaces, bracelets, and earrings. "See if you find anything you like there, while I take this dress off the model."

"Oh, I'd hate for you to go to all that trouble. Don't you have any on the rack?"

The proprietress looked scandalized. "Mademoiselle, everything in my shop is one of a kind." She smiled wryly. "And, of course, is priced accordingly."

Helene clapped her hands. "Don't worry. I'm willing to pay for the privilege of being the only one in the room wearing this beautiful gown."

Somewhat mollified, the store owner said, "That's as it should be, Mademoiselle. Now, can I interest you in any shoes? And what about a wrap?"

An hour later, Helene was struggling home beneath a

load of boxes. Despite her burden, she was wearing a huge grin. Not only had she found the perfect dress for Margot's movie premiere, the shopkeeper had created a whole fabulous look for her, making sure that every aspect of her outfit was just perfect. She'd even recommended what shade lipstick to wear. It made Helene feel as though she were a princess getting ready for the ball. A princess who wouldn't deign to be seen with a commoner like, for instance, Lazlo.

I wonder if Daniel D'Artois will be at the movie premiere? she thought as she stopped to catch a slipping box. I bet I wouldn't even need an introduction from Margot if he saw me wearing this dress. He'd send his spies to find out the name of the ravishing young lady in orange. She giggled to herself, stopping again to juggle her packages. Noticing the time on a bank clock, she quickened her steps. Dinner was in half an hour. Despite her lingering anger toward Alexis, she was still curious about her sister's first day at work.

Eight

The Gauntlet Is Thrown

"It was like something out of a movie," Alexis said as she helped herself to a generous portion of potage St-Germain (otherwise known as pea soup). "People running in and out with bolts of fabric. Boxes of sequins, feathers, and seed pearls everywhere you look. And the sketches! They're drawn everywhere—on notepads, napkins . . . even the walls! If somebody's got an idea, they run with it, even if it means drawing a picture on the mirror with lipstick, or pulling down the curtains to demonstrate how a dress should be draped. By the time I left, the studio looked like a tornado had hit."

"So much for Zen-like simplicity," Helene muttered.

Margot laughed. "Creative people can be messy people. I, myself, make it a rule never to tidy up when I am studying for a role. If my surroundings are too orderly, I become inhibited. My performance suffers."

Mr. Masterson smiled fondly at his wife. "Don't worry, darling. After you finish this next film, things will be a lot less chaotic. You'll finally be able to put some structure back into your life."

Helene's heart turned over. She wondered if her father had ever looked at her mother that way. She'd been so young when they divorced that she couldn't really remember any good times, just the long, stony silences that led to their inevitable separation. To look at him now, you'd never know he'd ever had another wife. Are all men this fickle? she wondered, thinking, once again, of Lazlo. I wonder what he's doing . . . and who he's doing it with. For the first time since she'd arrived in France, Helene wasn't hungry. She longed to confide in Alexis, to take back all the mean things she'd said. And she would have, if her sister had seemed even the least bit sad about their fight. Instead, she was acting as though it didn't faze her at all.

Margot looked at Alexis with a distinctly maternal expression. It made Helene ill.

"I'm glad the job has turned out so well," Margot said. "I do hope, however, that you won't focus entirely on work while you are here. Paris has so many wonderful diversions for a beautiful girl like yourself. And let us not forget the handsome men." She actually winked at Alexis.

Alexis smiled and said, "As a matter of fact, I've noticed that myself. In fact, there's one exceptionally handsome man I met today at Vedette."

Mr. Masterson laughed. "That was fast work. What's his name?"

Alexis looked Helene in the eye and said, "His name is Daniel."

Margot obviously thought highly of Alexis, but even she regarded this announcement with slightly raised eyebrows. Helene found herself wondering if Margot was only slightly interested, or if BOTOX injections had deadened the movement in her stepmother's face. You're never too young to worry about wrinkles—especially in Margot's line of work.

"Not Daniel D'Artois?"

Alexis was still looking at Helene when she spoke.

"*Oui.*"

After a short, strained silence, Margot suddenly threw back her head and laughed. "My dear, I applaud you. Two days in Paris and already you have your sights on its most eligible—and desirable—bachelor. Daniel D'Artois. *Mon dieu,* Trevor, imagine whom she'll go after when she graduates high school!"

The blood rushed to Helene's face. Alexis must really be angry to set her sights on Daniel, she thought, with a sinking feeling in her stomach. At the end of last summer, they'd both agreed never to go after the same boy again. It had been an easy decision, after wasting seven weeks fighting over somebody who turned out to be an arrogant jerk. (No matter that he was heir to the British throne, and that they'd never met him—he was still a jerk.) Now, apparently, Alexis was declaring all truces null and void, and that Daniel D'Artois was fair game for both of them.

A burst of laughter pulled Helene from her thoughts. Alexis and Margot were sharing some secret joke, while Mr. Masterson looked on indulgently. It was too much to bear. *First Alexis drops me like a hot potato, then she becomes best buddies with my stepmother. And now she's trying to steal my almost-boyfriend!*

Plastering a big, fake smile on her face, Helene suddenly announced that she had found a dress for Margot's big movie premiere.

"Honey, that's wonderful," Mr. Masterson cheered. Then, turning to Alexis, he asked, "Would you like to go with us? We could easily get an extra ticket."

"I'm afraid I won't be able to," Alexis explained. "I'll be too busy with work."

"But it's only one evening," Mr. Masterson said. "We'd love to have you join us."

"Oh, you won't miss me at all—not with a woman like Margot on your arm."

Mr. Masterson laughed. "Easy, Alexis. Margot already likes you, you don't have to work so hard."

Now Helene said sweetly, "Oh, don't pay any attention to Lexy. She's famous for sucking up to people, then stabbing them in the back."

Alexis shot Helene a look of disbelief as Mr. Masterson demanded, "What's going on here? Why are you girls fighting? I thought you were best friends."

Alexis smiled sweetly. "Of *course* we are, Mr. Masterson. Helene and I are just kidding around." She gave Helene a nudge beneath the table.

Helene yanked her leg away and said, "Yes, Daddy. It's just our way of showing affection for each other. Part of the, ah, *responsibility* of being stepsisters. Don't pay any attention."

Bewildered, Mr. Masterson said, "In that case, I'm glad the two of you won't be attending the premiere together. The press might mistake your affection for a catfight."

"If it makes you feel better, Daddy, I promise not to quarrel with Alexis at the dinner table anymore. I remember how your fights with Mom upset your digestion," Helene said in her best good-girl voice.

"Yes, Mr. Masterson, I'd certainly hate to disturb your enjoyment of dinner, especially now that you've managed to create such a wonderful home life," Alexis said, fluttering her eyelashes.

With that, everybody got up to leave the table.

If Helene hadn't been so angry, she would have

noticed her sister's lower lip quivering with emotion. For despite her wonderful job, despite her plan to introduce Daniel and Helene, Alexis was miserable. How could she not be, when her best friend thought she was a lying backstabber? Perhaps Alexis should have told Helene that she wasn't after Daniel for herself. But the insult hurt her so much that she didn't. She even considered, for a fleeting moment, doing exactly what her sister accused her of—stealing Daniel D'Artois.

If Alexis hadn't been so angry, she would have seen how the vein in Helene's forehead was throbbing. For despite her relaxing afternoon, despite her gorgeous evening gown, Helene felt wretched. How could it be otherwise, when her best friend thought she was a selfish pig?

Nine

The Beginning of a Beautiful Friendship?

That Friday was Margot's big movie premiere, and Alexis was working late. As tempting as it was to get a glimpse of the French film industry, she had other business to attend to. Namely, working her way into Daniel D'Artois's good graces—and him into her stepsister's arms.

She had hoped to see him that morning, but he spent most of the day in a meeting with his father. Rumor had it that Alain D'Artois was getting ready to retire and was anxious to show his son every aspect of the business before he officially left Vedette. From the way all the designers talked, though, it sounded as though Daniel was more interested in designing dresses rather than selling them, which is why he spent so much time in the studio. If that was the case, Alexis knew it was only a matter of time before they crossed paths. That alone would have been enough inducement to put in extra hours at the office. But the fact was, Alexis really liked her job and would have stayed late even if there was no chance of running into the man the tabloids had dubbed "the Prince of Paris."

Alexis's fellow interns didn't share her dedication. It was a Friday night, and they'd left en masse at 7:00 to start *le weekend*. After they were gone, the design studio was eerily quiet, so Alexis switched on the radio. She wheeled out a dress mannequin and knelt down to pin the hem of that morning's creation, a sea-blue sheath, elegantly draped in front, cascading into soft folds toward the floor. She was so intent on her work that her heart stopped in terror when she heard a deep male voice behind her.

"I thought I was the only one who worked late on Friday nights."

Alexis let out a shriek. Unfortunately, her mouth was full of straight pins, which scattered wildly. It was a miracle she didn't swallow one.

"Don't come any closer!" she yelled, brandishing pinking shears at her attacker. The first thing Alexis noticed was his eyes. Electric blue, peering out from a pair of battered horn-rimmed glasses, one arm of which was held in place with a safety pin. It was a long moment before she could tear her gaze from his and take in the rest of him: curly brown hair, great cheekbones, a slim but solid build. The stranger held up his hands now in mock surrender.

"Okay, I give up. Only please, watch where you point those things."

For a second, Alexis remained frozen. Then she was overcome with laughter. "I am *so* sorry," she managed to gasp. "But you scared me!"

The young man offered her a hand up. "No, I should apologize. I thought you heard me come in."

Alexis stood up and shook her head, gesturing to the mannequin. "I was too wrapped up in my work. I wanted to finish this dress before I went home."

The man took a step back and frowned critically. Then he stepped forward and began circling the mannequin. "Nice," he said. "Very nice, in fact. You have real talent."

"Thanks. What's your name?"

"Philippe Martin. What's yours?"

"Alexis Worth. You work here?"

Philippe nodded. "I'm the photography intern. Next year I'm going to university to study film but, you know, you can learn a lot about framing and composition from stills."

Alexis laughed. "All the models and beautiful clothes must make it a little easier."

Philippe smirked back at her. "After eighteen months

of perfect cheekbones and pouty lips, you don't really notice them anymore. I've been developing since noon. . . . I had no idea it had gotten so late. By the time I left the darkroom, everyone else had gone home. At least, I thought everyone had gone home until I saw the light from your studio."

Alexis glanced toward the clock. "I guess it *is* kind of late. Maybe I should get going."

"Would you care to join me for dinner?" Seeing her hesitate, Philippe added, "You can bring the scissors, if you want. But I assure you, I'm too tired to launch an attack. At least until I have a coffee."

Alexis giggled. "All right, I'll join you. But, remember, if you try any funny business, I've got this seam ripper aimed right at your heart."

Delighted to find a kindred spirit, Philippe's eyes lit up. "That, my dear, is my least vulnerable spot."

"It's so nice to have a friend in Paris," Alexis said, sipping her cappuccino at a sidewalk table of a small café. "Work's been great and everything, but I haven't had much time for fun since I arrived."

She and Philippe were sitting on the avenue Matignon, which was just down the street from Vedette. It was a casual, noisy spot filled with rough wooden tables and bustling waiters. The patrons were mostly young students who sat sipping wine and smoking cigarettes for hours at a time. After last night's tumultuous dinner at Chez Masterson, Alexis welcomed the laid-back atmosphere.

Despite having just met him, she felt an easy camaraderie with Philippe. Kind of like the one she used to feel with Helene, before they got into their horrendous fight.

"No wonder you had a hard time getting acquainted with people," said Philippe, sipping his after-dinner coffee. "Threatening a total stranger with a pair of scissors isn't exactly the best way to break the ice. Still, it reminded me of the movies, very Tracy meets Hepburn, or Bogart meets Bacall."

"Or Jason meets Freddy?" Alexis inquired.

"Yes, something like that. Though I wouldn't call it one of my favorite films."

"Not many people would," Alexis laughed. "You know, it's because of the movies that I learned French."

Philippe raised his eyebrows. "Really?"

She began making little rips around the perimeter of her cocktail napkin. "Well, it's kind of dumb, actually. When I was a little girl, Vanessa—that's my mother—took me to see *Gigi*. And I absolutely fell in love with it. I didn't understand the plot at all . . . too grown up for a seven-year-old girl. Still, I loved how the movie transported me to this city that seemed like something out of a dream." Alexis drew a deep breath and looked to gauge Philippe's reaction. "Is this making any sense to you?"

"Perfect sense. Go on."

"When we left the theater, I told my mother I wanted to live in Paris when I grew up. She told me, 'Then you'll have to learn French, dear, because that's what everyone there speaks.' She was kind of laughing at me when she said it, and it made me mad. So I said, 'Okay, I *will* learn it.' And I did."

Philippe regarded her intently. "I think that's the best reason for learning a foreign language I've ever heard."

She laughed nervously. "I don't know. Lots of Americans think learning a different language is a waste of time, because English is spoken in so many places."

Philippe shook his head vigorously. "I suppose that's true, but French remains the language of love."

"Speaking of love . . ." Alexis paused clumsily. Normally, she'd find a more graceful way to broach the topic, but time was of the essence. Summer would be over before she knew it. "How well do you know Daniel?"

"Daniel D'Artois?" Philippe raised an eyebrow. "Not well, really. Only that he's in line to inherit a couture house to which his father devoted his life. Let's hope he's up to the task."

Alexis frowned slightly. "You sound . . . skeptical?" She'd almost said jealous but didn't think that would make a great impression on her first Parisian friend.

Philippe shrugged. "Daniel certainly has great passion for fashion. He works hard, and he pays attention to people's taste. But his father"—Philippe's strong hands grasped at something ineffable a couple of feet above the café table—"his father is a genius. The kind of man whose name can be said in the same breath with that of Laurent or Lacroix or even Chanel. It is a heavy mantle for anyone to assume, and Daniel . . ." Philippe let his voice trail off, seeming to sense that his words weren't meeting a warm reception. "What do I know, I'm just an aspiring filmmaker, and Daniel is—what do they call him?—the Prince of Paris."

Alexis struggled not to blush, but felt her cheeks grow warm anyway. "Don't misunderstand me, Philippe. I'm not a snob . . . it's just that I'd like to know a little more about him because—"

"Because he's handsome and famous and single?" Philippe interrupted dryly. "Well, I can hardly blame you. But you should remember that Daniel D'Artois will inherit one of the most important fashion houses in France. Fashion, wine, and philosophy are France's national obsessions, and in Paris, fashion is queen." Philippe smiled wryly. "When he marries, his wife will be forced to remain in the wings. I wonder if you are the kind of girl who could do that."

"Marriage?" Alexis said huffily. "Who's talking about marriage?"

"I'm afraid there is no such thing as casual dating for Daniel D'Artois. You see, he has been raised to protect his interests at all times. He has been taught to avoid fortune hunters."

"Philippe!" Alexis suddenly laughed. "If we hadn't just met, I'd swear you are jealous!"

"I'm not jealous," he answered, looking down at his hands and blushing.

"And I'm not interested in Daniel D'Artois—not for myself, at least. I had hoped to hook him up with my sister, who—and you can quote me on this—is no fortune hunter."

"Oh?" Philippe looked up at Alexis and smiled. "In that case, he seems like a really nice guy."

Just then, there was a commotion at the tables to their right. A tiny Pomeranian snapped at a hulking German shepherd mix. The owners glared balefully at each other. Finally, the woman with the Pomeranian agreed to move to another table, muttering angrily the whole time. The man with the shepherd blew her a kiss, then sent over a bottle of wine.

Eager to change the subject, Alexis said, "Well that's a good thing to see. People don't seem to be able to stay angry at each other for long."

Philippe adjusting his eyeglasses. "The Hundred Years' War was hardly brief. I take it you're not a student of history?"

She winced. "No, that's Helene, the sister I just mentioned. You'd probably like her; she's the intellectual one. She's always talking about history, art, and culture. Strictly Left Bank. Me, I'm a philistine."

"Anybody who speaks French as well as you can't possibly be a philistine," said Philippe. "You obviously appreciate film and, judging from your work at the design studio, you have an eye for beauty. Do you know what I think?"

Alexis had never heard herself summed up so baldly. All she could do was shake her head.

"I think you're much more sensitive than you pretend. Somewhere along the line, you learned to hide your feelings beneath a cool, calculating exterior. Perhaps your visit to Paris will convince you that there's no harm in expressing your emotions, especially among friends." Philippe covered her hand with his, then quickly drew it away, as if embarrassed. "I'm sorry. I hardly know you. You must think I'm horribly forward."

"No, I don't. I'll tell you what I *do* think, though."

"What?"

"That this could be the beginning of a beautiful friendship."

Ten

I Think, Therefore I'm Glam

Helene sat stock still on the jump seat of the limousine, trying not to wrinkle her tangerine dress. It had taken her over two hours to get ready for Margot's premiere, but the results were worth it. Following the shopkeeper's suggestion, she had chosen to wear a neutral color on her lips and play up her big, prominent eyes. She had swept her long, curly hair into a loose chignon to make her round face look more angular. An emerald necklace improved the effect. Glancing into the mirror of her compact, Helene couldn't help but feel gratified at her appearance. She had never looked lovelier, and she knew it.

Margot and her father were seated directly across from her. Mr. Masterson kept shifting around nervously, checking his watch and straightening the tie of his tuxedo. He kept asking Margot if she was all right, but Helene suspected that he was on the verge of a nervous breakdown. She couldn't blame him: A huge crowd had gathered outside the car. The screams and cheers grew louder and louder as the minutes ticked by.

Margot seemed oblivious to the whole scene. Finally, she called out, *"Maintenant, Pierre."* The chauffeur put down his copy of *Men Are from Mars, Women Are from Venus* and ran to open her door. Turning to her husband, she said, "Follow me. Make sure not to fall more than three steps behind." The door opened, and Margot stepped into a sea of warm, dazzling light. Mr. Masterson and Helene followed.

The first few steps down the red carpet (*"le tapis rouge,"* as Margot called it), were positively terrifying. Flashbulbs popped, reporters shouted, and fans screamed. Helene felt as though she were being pulled into a giant ocean. Swimming against the tide was futile; a crush of press agents kept prodding her toward the entrance of the movie theater. It seemed to Helene that her father was equally helpless. Only Margot appeared fully in charge of the situation. Every sixteen steps— Helene, whose eyes were fastened to Margot's Sigerson Morrison slingbacks, found herself counting them to keep from hyperventilating—Margot paused for the photographers, making it look as though she were doing so at the special request of one of the fans on the other side of the velvet rope. She refused to sign any autographs, though; one time she held up her freshly manicured hands, adorned only by her platinum wedding band and the large diamond on her engagement ring, as though to say that such delicate, beautiful hands could never be sullied by something as quotidian as a mere *pen*. Helene had to admit her stepmother wasn't merely beautiful in the hot pink dress with a plunging back she'd bought for the occasion, but almost regal in her supreme poise, although not exactly warm. Beside her, Mr. Masterson's shiny face beamed like a lightbulb, his expression somewhere between that of doting husband and freshly fed puppy. Helene felt like a third wheel and wondered why on earth she'd ever thought anyone would notice her, new dress or not.

But then, suddenly, someone did notice her. Some reporters started shouting questions her way. Of course, she understood almost no French—*"Comment t'appelle tu, mademoiselle?"* was about all she was able to pick out—but they seemed friendly. Helene blushed, smiled, and waved to the cameras. Disappointed by Margot's lofty but slightly chilly reception, her fans began to shout their approval of Helene, thrusting autograph books into her hand. She shrugged and laughed, scribbling her name onto the scraps of paper. Seeing the commotion, Margot's manager stopped to investigate and found Helene surrounded by admirers. He snarled something in French, then shoved her out of the circle. Fans booed. Helene meekly made her way toward the entrance, but not before making a mocking face at the manager once his back was turned. The crowed cheered and clapped, and several photographers were quick enough to capture the face on film.

By the time she entered Le Grand Rex movie theater, Helene was flush with happiness. "Where have you been?" Margot asked sourly, then flounced away before her stepdaughter had a chance to answer. Mr. Masterson followed anxiously. Helene felt a pang in her heart.

The three made their way to the front of the theater, settling themselves in seats covered with plush red velvet. Helene paused to admire her surroundings. The movie house was one of those old-fashioned kinds with a cathedral ceiling, ornate woodwork, and gilded wall sconces. The plump red chairs were newly upholstered, and as Helene thought of her favorite multiplex back home, she figured she'd take Old World elegance over stadium seating any day. How could any movie *not* look good in such a magical environment? As much as she liked the theater, however, she couldn't stop herself from making a sarcastic comment.

"What," she said quietly to her father as they got comfortable, "no cup holders built into the armrests? What kind of theater is this?"

Trevor Masterson laughed at his daughter's joke, but Margot merely glanced coldly at her, then turned to a pair of women in the aisle and began conversing with them in rapid French.

"This is Paris, honey," Helene's father said to her as they took their seats. "They'd have to make holders for wineglasses."

Helene looked at her father lovingly. It was the first casual moment they'd shared since she arrived, and she thought it was funny that it should come in such extravagant surroundings.

"Thanks for bringing me here, Dad."

"Don't thank me, thank Margot. It's her party."

Helene refused to let the mention of her stepmother's name dampen her mood.

"I don't mean the premiere. I mean to Paris. It's good to spend time with my dad." And she leaned over and gave her father a little kiss on the cheek.

Mr. Masterson practically misted up.

"There's no doubt I'm the luckiest guy in the room tonight. Seated between the two most beautiful women here. That dress looks beautiful on you, honey."

Now it was Helene's turn to mist up. She soared on a euphoria that couldn't even be dampened by Margot squeezing into the aisle and immediately drawing Mr. Masterson's attention away from his daughter. Instead, she began to examine the crowd. Many of the men were in tuxedos, but most wore smart-looking suits, while the women sported dresses of every color and description. French men seemed to put more effort into their appearance than American guys, while French women didn't seem so intent on hiding their age. Craning her head around the room, Helene couldn't see one ugly plastic surgery job in the crowd. At home, she was always running into middle-aged women whose faces looked painfully tight and young girls with disproportionately tiny noses. It made her feel good to see sixty-year-old women who looked their age and girls her own age who didn't surgically alter their imperfections.

Then again, the French clearly admired flawless beauty, as evidenced by the throngs of fans who came out to cheer Margot. Of course, they might have been here because of her stepmother's acting talent, but Helene wasn't in the mood to be charitable just then. Once the lights dimmed and the movie began, though, she began to change her mind.

The movie was called *Cinq à Sept*. It was about a couple who had been married for five years and were now bored with each other. Instead of going to counseling or getting a divorce, they decided to "take a vacation" from their relationship between the hours of five and seven every evening. Helene blushed crimson as she watched her stepmother's sex scenes with the hot young actor who played her lover. She was glad the darkness of the theater covered her embarrassment. She had a distinct feeling that if Margot saw her horrified expression it would not go over well, and the last thing Helene wanted was to appear even more unsophisticated in front of her stepmother.

Glancing to her left, she noticed she wasn't the only one in the audience who seemed embarrassed. Several times her father shifted awkwardly in his seat and looked away from the screen. Margot was too intent on watching the movie to see her husband's reaction. Despite all the steamy on-screen action, Helene had to admit that her stepmother was a good actress. Maybe even a great one. She became really choked up during the final scene, when the husband and wife confront each other's infidelities and decide they can't repair their marriage. At home, Margot was nearly emotionless, but on the screen, she was able to cry as though her heart would break. Which is the real Margot? Helene wondered, as she noticed her stepmother quickly touching a handkerchief to each eye before the lights went up. Straightening her shoulders, she stood to acknowledge the crowd, which burst into applause. Margot basked in the spotlight, seeming to draw strength from it.

Mr. Masterson, on the other hand, looked as though he couldn't wait to get out of the theater. He grabbed his coat and held it to his torso like a shield, then began pushing his way down the aisle. Helene quickly followed, stumbling over people's feet and muttering apologies along the way. Looking over her shoulder, she saw Margot look toward them with a hurt expression. Instead of racing to follow her family, she lifted her head and gave a slight smile to the crowd, which responded with a roar of approval.

"Dad, wait up," Helene called, fighting to keep up with the retreating figure before her. Mr. Masterson didn't seem to be listening. He took long, purposeful strides up the aisle and out of the theater. By the time Helene reached his side, he was already at the corner, hailing a taxi. "Daddy, where are you going? We're supposed to go to the party with Margot, remember?"

"Helene, I'm going home. I've got a splitting headache. You take the limo to the party. I'm just not feeling up to it."

"But, Dad," Helene said. She thought about Margot's proud face as she turned to acknowledge the cheers of the crowd. Then she remembered the smirks, silences, and put-downs she'd endured ever since coming to Paris.

"Yes, baby, what is it?" Her father looked as though he'd aged ten years since they first arrived at the premiere.

"Feel better. I'll see you in the morning."

"Nice try. I want you home no later than midnight. I'll

be waiting up." He slammed the door of the taxi and it sped off toward Chez Masterson.

Pierre pulled up in the limo as the taxi disappeared into traffic. Looking around, Helene realized that Margot was nowhere in sight. For a split second, she wondered if she should wait for her stepmother. Then she caught a glimpse of herself in the side mirror, resplendent in all of her finery. You'd better take this coach now, Cinderella, before it turns into a pumpkin. She jumped into the backseat and cried to the driver, "Pierre, take me to the party!"

Pierre swiveled his neck and asked in a worried voice, *"Où est Madame Masterson? Nous ne pouvons pas partir sans elle."*

Helene laughed. "Cut it out, Pierre. I know you speak English. Now take me to the party unless you want to make my father very, very angry."

The driver slumped in his seat. "Call me Pete," he said in a thick Boston accent. "What gave me away?" he asked, pulling away from the curb.

"Actually, it was your reading material," Helene said as they sped off to the party. "Why did you pretend not to speak English?"

Pete glanced apologetically in the rear view mirror. "When I realized you didn't speak French and then you asked me about your stepmother, I just figured playing dumb was the best way to go. Getting mixed up in your employer's family affairs is a good way to lose your job."

"Lucky for you, you don't have to get mixed up in them," Helene said, thinking about her fight with Alexis and, then, how unhappy her father had looked when he left minutes earlier. Still there was a party to go to and nothing she could do about her father or Alexis now. She leaned forward in her seat. "All right, Pete, let's go. Maybe on the way you can tell me about that great book you're reading."

"This?" Pete asked, holding up the book. "I'm sure you'd find it petty boring."

"I doubt it," she said, grinning as the car pulled off. "And especially not on the night I intend to find my Prince Charming. Who knows, he might even be from Mars!"

The party was held at Divan du Monde, a cool club in Montmartre. House music pumped from a DJ booth in the back corner. Low lights invited romantic couples to linger in the corners. The long bar was jammed with people three deep, trying to be heard over the music. At last, Helene was getting a taste of Parisian nightlife.

Margot arrived at the party shortly after she did. "Where is your father?" she snarled, digging her nails into Helene's arm. "We were supposed to come to the party together."

"Daddy said he had a headache, and to go ahead without him," Helene answered. "Pierre and I waited and waited, but we didn't see you anywhere. I thought you might have gotten a ride with somebody else. Sorry about the mix-up." She widened her eyes in an attempt to look innocent, but she could tell Margot wasn't fooled.

Her stepmother stomped off to a small corner table and sat down by herself. An eager fan leaped forward to greet her, only to be dismissed with an angry wave of the hand. Nobody else dared approach. After a few solitary minutes, Margot got up and left without saying good-bye to her.

For once, Helene was too distracted to care about her stepmother's behavior. Everywhere she turned, people were introducing themselves to her, apparently eager to meet the pretty American in tangerine. People were even more excited when they learned that Helene was, in fact, Margot's stepdaughter. "Do you wish to become an actress yourself?" a reporter asked, his pencil poised over his notepad.

Imagining her father's response to such a question, Helene let out a wicked laugh. The reporter looked confused, then she hurried to explain, "Oh no, it's just that acting is the last profession I'd ever consider. I mean, look at me!" she said, spreading her arms. "I'm almost twice the size of any actress my age!"

"In other words, you are perfectly proportioned," she heard a male voice say in a sexy French accent.

Helene turned to look into the most beautiful pair of eyes she had ever seen. *Wow, he looks familiar,* she thought, then caught sight of his perfectly chiseled noise. "Daniel D'Artois!" she exclaimed, once she figured out who he was, then immediately wished a hole would open beneath her so that she could fall through it.

Daniel smiled. "At your service. I feel ashamed to be at such a disadvantage, though. You know my name, but I don't know yours."

Helene giggled and extended her hand. "Pleased to make your acquaintance."

Daniel took her by the elbow and steered her into a booth upholstered in red leather. Helene noticed heads turning in their direction as he slid in next to her.

"I don't want to disappoint you, Daniel," she said, looking around the room self-consciously, "but I'm here visiting my father, and he told me to be home by midnight. It's already after two A.M. I expect to be sent packing the moment I get home."

"Parents can sometimes be difficult," he answered.

"What would you know about that?" Helene asked. "You're father's one of the coolest men in Paris."

"I'd hardly call him 'cool,' though certainly his dresses are very popular," Daniel said, shaking his head. "Believe me, he can be as difficult as any father. Growing up, he had all sorts of expectations of me. Last year, he finally realized that these expectations were highly unrealistic, that we are two separate people. Probably your own father will come to the same realization."

"I hope you're right."

"It is never easy for fathers to see their daughters growing into women. All my life, I have been surrounded by young ladies. Always I hear them complain. From birth to the age of thirteen, their fathers have been their greatest champion. Then, these girls turn into young women. And the fathers do not like it."

Helene said grouchily, "Well, what are we supposed to turn into? Pumpkins? Besides, my father should be the last one to complain. He's married to Margot Morganne, for crying out loud! The woman's practically half his age."

Daniel shook his head sadly. "Ah, but then you should take pity on him. Because the girlish devotion of a young wife is not destined to last. Eventually, the wife, too, grows up. It is a precious thing, the love of a daughter. Most men do not understand that it can also be a fleeting thing."

Helene threw up her hands. "So what should I do?"

"One day, your father will no longer see you as a small girl, seeking his approval. He will discover a beautiful, self-possessed woman, and be proud of you."

Helene laughed. "Okay, so what's my next move? Run for president? Swim the English Channel? Invent a cure for cancer?"

"I was wondering whether you would consider becoming a model for my father's fashion house."

Helene sat in stunned silence. Then she said in a small voice, "You know, I thought you were a nice guy, the way we were just sitting here, talking. Now I realize that you're just like all men . . . totally insensitive!" She got up from the table, nearly overturning it in her haste to get away.

Daniel reached up and grabbed her arm. "Stop . . . don't go! What have I done to upset you?"

"Don't you think I realize that I'm no model? That I'm tired of being told that it's more important to have a good sense of humor than a gorgeous face? Well, apparently I've got neither, because I fail to see the humor in offering me a modeling job!"

Daniel pulled her back down into the booth. "I'm afraid there has been a great misunderstanding. You see, I never joke about business. My offer was a serious one. You *are* beautiful, and I want you to be the new face of Vedette."

Helene's mouth dropped open. Fighting to regain her poise, she asked, "And what would 'the new face of Vedette' be expected to do?"

Daniel stepped in close, one hand outstretched. For a moment, Helene thought he was actually going to kiss her, but instead he put his hand on her chin and gently turned her face toward a mirror. "All you have to do," Daniel whispered huskily in her ear, "is look like that."

Helene looked in the mirror. In the background were the flashing lights and the glamorous partygoers, laughing, dancing, gesturing wildly with cigarettes and wineglasses (without ever spilling a drop!), but in the center of the frame there was just she—she and Daniel. He had stepped to one side so she could see herself better, and one of his arms rested lightly on her bare shoulders; on his face was a little bit of the expression she had seen on her father's face earlier, when he'd looked at his wife on the red carpet. She was so focused on the way Daniel was looking at her that she almost forgot to look at herself, but when she did, finally, she almost gasped. It was true. She was beautiful. Her curves, her coloring, but most importantly her sense of herself. She didn't have to stand in any woman's shadow—not Alexis's, not Margot's.

"You see it, don't you?" Daniel said, and in the mirror she saw him smile. "It is a wonderful thing when a woman first discovers her own beauty."

It was all so perfect. And yet why did Helene see a different face in the mirror next to hers for just one moment—not Daniel's, but Lazlo's. For a second, Helene saw herself at Heathrow Airport, flying into Lazlo's arms (still in the orange dress, of course), but then the image dissolved in favor of the one before her eyes—which was, after all, every bit as much of a fairy tale, only it was real. What am I *doing*? Helene thought. I'm standing next to France's most eligible bachelor and all I can think of is some guy who can't be bothered to write me back?

She found Daniel's eyes in the mirror and smiled into them. "I believe we are destined for great things together."

"Wonderful! Then only one question remains. I hope you don't think it's too bold."

Helene looked wary. What if he asks me to do some 'test modeling' back at his place? "Well, go ahead and ask."

"'Mademoiselle' sounds too formal. What should I call you?"

She realized then she hadn't even told him her name.

Eleven

Back to the Drawing Board

The following Monday, Alexis was sitting glumly at her desk in the basement of Maison Vedette, her sketches spread before her like an oversized deck of cards. Last week she'd been so inspired by her own creativity that she'd actually forgotten about Margot's premiere. The designs had practically poured out of her onto the page. Her fellow interns had been even more impressed by her drawings than by her French—and when she'd told them she'd never even studied fashion, they shook their heads and refused to believe it. But today her drawings looked like a child's coloring book to her, and with an exasperated sigh, she shuffled them together and closed the cover of her pad. All that hard work for nothing, she thought.

Helene had announced her modeling job Saturday morning, sailing into Chez Masterson just as the family was settling down to breakfast. She could barely keep the pride out of her voice, especially when she recited Daniel's comments on her beauty. Alexis had expected her sister to get punished for staying out all night, but Mr. Masterson and Margot didn't say a word about it. In fact, they barely said a word to each other as Helene related the events of previous evening.

Alexis seethed with fury the entire weekend. First her sister had accused her of going back on their promise to never again chase the same boy, and now Helene was stealing her thunder at Vedette, too. Alexis would spend the rest of the summer chained to her desk—in the basement!—while her sister not only had the time of her life with the most eligible bachelor in town, but got her picture in magazines to boot. Life, seventeen-year-old Alexis Worth thought to herself, was just not fair.

Sighing again, she flipped open her drawing pad and turned to the first blank page. What would Daniel put Helene in? she wondered. Something colorful, no doubt. Tight at the waist, a little low in the neckline, to accentuate her sister's best features. Her pencil moved idly over the page. Something quirky, asymmetrical, maybe. A single strap on the dress? Or the hemline, cut on the bias? Maybe both. Alexis drew with more purpose now. Helene was always punking herself out, distorting the shape of her body with baggy cargo pants and combat boots. It was a miracle she'd managed to pick out that orange dress to wear to the premiere—it really was just the right thing for her. Daniel would design dresses like that for her. Dresses for women with personality, who didn't want to look like everyone else who shopped at the mall.

Sometime later, a shadow fell over her drawing pad, and without looking up Alexis said, "My light. You're in my light. I'm trying to get just the right shading on this skirt, and it's dark enough in this dung—"

Her voice broke off when she looked up to Daniel D'Artois, who regarded her with an amused smirk on his face. "Dung—?"

Alexis wracked her brain for a positive word that started with "dung." If such a word existed, she couldn't find it. But before she could stammer an excuse, Daniel had reached out and taken her drawing pad from her.

"What lovely sketches," he said. "Your lines are so graceful and fluid, a refreshing departure from all the geometric shapes we've seen the past few seasons." The spicy smell of Daniel's cologne enveloped Alexis like a warm, hypnotic cloud. He paused at the final sketch—the dress Alexis had drawn for Helene—and traced his finger over her sister's hip. Fortunately, she hadn't drawn Helene's face. "Tell me," Daniel said now. "What goes into your designs?"

"My designs?" Alexis said confusedly. "Oh, my *designs*. Yes, well, I've been thinking a lot about . . . uh . . . the human form. And how clothes should accentuate the body, not mask it." She willed herself to look into his gorgeous gray eyes, which seemed to be laughing at her. She became aware that the busy whirlwind of activity that normally characterized the design studio had slowed to a virtual standstill. Everybody seemed to find excuses to walk by her table.

After the fifth intern came to borrow a pencil, Daniel smiled and said, "I see we are afforded very little privacy here. Would you care to join me for lunch this afternoon? I would like to discuss a little project I have in mind."

She nodded dumbly. Lunch with the boss. How could she turn that down? I hope he takes me someplace expensive, she thought, then gave a guilty start.

"Is there something wrong?" Daniel asked, noting her discomfort.

"Wrong? Oh no, not at all! I was just wondering . . . if I'm suitably dressed to go out. I'd planned to eat in the park this afternoon."

Daniel looked at her pretty yellow dress appreciatively. "You have nothing to fear, my dear. What you are wearing is perfect."

No wonder he has a reputation for being a heartbreaker, Alexis thought. Helene better watch her step with him. It's one thing to go after a guy for the summer; it's another to fall in love with Casanova!

They exited the darkened design studio, out into the

hot Paris sunshine. The sky overhead was bright blue, and people were promenading along the streets as though they hadn't a care in the world. Alexis watched wistfully, aware that she was spending most of her summer vacation in an office building. Granted, it was one of the most glamorous fashion houses in the world, but it was still an office. She thought about Helene, who would be spending her days posing on fashion shoots. She turned to Daniel.

"You know, I've been so focused on my job that I've hardly had any time to explore the city."

Daniel looked at her gravely. "Paris is filled with many amusements, but where I'm about to take you is a place of worship."

Alexis's smile became a little fixed. "Oh, I didn't realize you were religious."

"Yes, like most French people, I pause to give thanks to my creator each afternoon." They passed a couple who was passionately making out.

"So I guess we'll grab something to eat afterward?" Alexis asked weakly, remembering her meager breakfast of coffee and rolls.

Daniel turned down the avenue des Champs-Elysées, and Alexis tried to match her long strides to his. It was hard, in high heels, on cobblestones. Not hard to keep up, but to look graceful while doing so.

Finally, Daniel came to a halt in front of an elegant restaurant. With a sweeping arm gesture, he said, "Mademoiselle Worth, welcome to church. As always, Chef Pierre Gagnaire will be presiding over the service."

Alexis giggled with relief. "I've been to lots of restaurants in my time, but never to one that was worthy of worship." They entered an elegant blue and silver dining room whose patrons were just as stylish as the decor. The maître d' stepped forward casually, but Alexis noticed that he bypassed several people ahead of them to speak to Daniel. "Monsieur D'Artois, always a pleasure to see you."

Daniel gave him a double kiss. "Do you have a quiet spot for me and my companion? We'd like to discuss business."

The maître d' smiled knowingly. "Of course, monsieur. Right this way." Then, turning on his heel, he led Daniel and Alexis past the loud hubbub of the dining salon, to a quieter room in the back.

After they'd been seated, a gorgeous waiter came to pour their water. Alexis, used to being admired wherever she went, was a little discouraged when he focused all of his attention on Daniel, vowing to "bring those hors d'oeuvres that monsieur enjoyed so much on his last visit." It seemed to Alexis that they were talking in a sort of code, but for the life of her, she couldn't crack it.

"Do you know what you'd like?" Daniel said to her.

Alexis noticed that he hadn't even looked at his menu and, smiling brightly, put hers to one side.

"You obviously know what's good here. Would you mind ordering for me?"

As they made their way through a glorious meal of foie gras and dried figs, baby artichokes in Jerusalem cream, and truffled lasagna, Daniel quizzed her about her concept of style. It was fun holding forth about the difference between fads and fashion. By the time dessert came (a luscious chocolate mousse atop which floated a cloud of whipped cream so light and airy that she could almost pretend it had no calories), Alexis realized that they had been discussing work the entire time.

"So Daniel," she said, reaching for the silver vase of bluebells on the table. "What do you do in your spare time?"

Daniel smiled and wiped his lips with his napkin. "My life isn't nearly as glamorous as the newspapers would have you believe. Most of the time, I confer with my father, trying to learn the business, so that I can take over when he is ready to retire. Which brings me to the reason I asked you to lunch."

Alexis tingled with excitement. *Here it is, the moment of truth.*

"For the past ten years, French fashion houses have

been losing their edge. Chanel, Yves Saint Laurent, Givenchy . . . they've all lost ground to Italian and American designers. Even British companies are gaining on us. That Alexander McQueen." Daniel shuddered slightly at the thought of the rogue British designer. "I am determined this will not happen to Vedette. We need to update our image. Dressing rich society matrons is all well and good, but we need clothes that will appeal to girls your age. And your designs have that youthful quality I've been looking for. That dress I saw today—it was the kind of thing I imagine an American girl wearing to the movies."

Alexis blushed. "You decided this after seeing a few of my sketches?"

"I confess one of the photographers has been singing your praises."

"A photographer sang my praises? I didn't realize anyone at Vedette had noticed me."

Daniel nodded. "Philippe said he noticed your work as he was leaving the office Friday night. He has a marvelous eye for beauty."

Philippe! Alexis's stomach took a curious lurch. She knew Philippe liked her designs, but enough to mention them to Daniel?

"I'd like you to help me create a very special dress for Vedette. It will serve as the centerpiece of a new clothing line that is being designed for younger girls. Is this something you would like to do?"

A millisecond of chagrin, followed by a huge wave of exaltation. "I'd love it! When do we start?" She imagined her dresses on the covers of fashion magazines, the praise and accolades from the press: another work of art by the talented, young designer, Alexis . . .

"Immediately," Daniel's voice, excited but businesslike, cut into her reverie. "But I haven't told you the best part. You see, I've found the perfect model to launch this new clothing line. She is wild, irreverent, and unconventional . . . all the things I want this line to be. I need you to meet her, so that you can get a feel for the desired style."

Her lips felt numb. "So, who is this mystery girl? Has she modeled for anyone else before?"

"That is the best part. She is totally unknown, my own discovery."

For a moment, Alexis drew a blank on the name. Daniel had pronounced it in the French manner, with a silent H.

"Ellen?"

"Helene Masterson," Daniel smiled at her. "With your help, she will be known all over the world."

Twelve

The Enlightenment

"Don't you dare ask me to make love to the camera," Helene warned. "As far as I'm concerned, we're barely on speaking terms."

It was her first photo shoot. She and Daniel and the camera crew had headed out to the Latin Quarter, where Helene posed in front of bookstalls, cafés, and jazz clubs, trying to look casual in a black lace top, lime green skirt, and diamond drop earrings. So far, the experience had been a dismal failure. No matter how often Daniel urged her to relax and be herself, Helene was always conscious of the camera. It was only when she paused to feed a scraggly group of pigeons that Philippe, the photographer, was able to take a few good shots.

Daniel shuddered. "How can you like such filthy creatures?"

Helene looked up, her face glowing. "I love all animals, I guess. They're so grateful for any kindness you show. Not like people." The photographer snapped another picture. "Gosh, haven't you had enough, already? You'd think this guy would get bored with taking my picture all the time."

"Philippe, why don't we take a break? Helene, may I speak to you a moment?" Daniel pulled her over to the side. "Remember, *chérie,* the whole purpose of our being here is to take your picture. As the face of Vedette, you must become accustomed to being photographed all the time, and not just by professionals. Once you become famous . . . and I feel that you will, very quickly . . . you will not be able to go anywhere without being recognized and photographed."

"Sounds fabulous," Helene gushed. Can't wait to give up my privacy for a bunch of fancy clothes that I'll never be able to wear out, anyway, she thought. Talk about being all dressed up with no place to go!

"Wait here a moment," Daniel said, "I need to speak with the others." He walked off to confer with the crew, allowing Helene to relax for the first time since they'd arrived, three hours ago. She gazed longingly at the open-air café across the street, where people were eating, reading, and talking with abandon. Seeing her reflection in the window of a boutique, she could barely recognize herself. It wasn't just the fancy clothes or the artful makeup job: It was the lonely look in her eyes.

Soon, Daniel was beside her again, a serious look on

his face. She saw the camera crew packing up its gear in the distance. "Anything wrong?" she asked, trying to sound as if she hadn't a care in the world.

"Nothing much. We just decided to call it a day and have an early dinner. Join me?" It was more of a command than a request.

This is your big chance, Helene told herself. Don't screw it up. She smiled pleasantly. "Of course. Where should we go?"

"Let's just step into this café for a moment. It was a great favorite of Ernest Hemingway, among others."

Helene's face glowed. "Oh, I love Hemingway! He's one of my favorite writers. Lazlo always teased me about it, saying what I really liked was his macho aggression. But really, I think he's a lot deeper than people give him credit for."

"And who is this Lazlo? Your boyfriend?"

Helene, you idiot! You're supposed to be seducing him, not blabbing about other guys! She gave a huge fake laugh. "Lazlo, my boyfriend? God, no. He's . . . uh . . . more of a . . . well, actually, he's my . . . pet psychic."

The two crossed the street and grabbed an outdoor table from a guy who was just leaving. The man gave Daniel a knowing smile, then sauntered off.

"Do you two know each other?" Helene asked, smoothing down her skirt.

"In a way. Paris is a much smaller city than it seems. Keep running into the same people if you frequent certain places." Daniel was intently studying the menu. "I think I will have a coffee."

Helene bounced in her seat. "I'm going to have one of those yummy cheese plates." The waiter approached.

"Deux cafés, ni lait, ni sucre." Daniel waved a disapproving finger at Helene. "Remember, now that you are a model, you must eat accordingly."

She slumped her shoulders. "I thought you said before I was perfectly proportioned."

"Your proportions may be perfect, but we must work to keep them that way." Daniel paused a minute before continuing. "I saw that you were having some difficulty today. It was hard for you to relax in front of the camera. For a young woman whose personal style seems to me to be all about garnering attention, you seemed strangely uncomfortable having people look at you."

The waiter deposited two coffees at their table, then moved away to attend to another table.

"It's just, I don't know," Helene began, not quite sure what she wanted to say. "Most days I just get up and throw some things on and don't even worry about what I look like."

Daniel laughed. "Yes, but coming from your closet, any ensemble is guaranteed to make an impression."

Helene wasn't sure what Daniel meant by that, but decided to take it as a compliment.

"I mean, sometimes I do spend a lot of time trying to look, you know, just so. Like at the premiere the other night. But most days, it's a miracle if I remember to comb my hair."

"You have beautiful hair, Helene. Combed or uncombed."

Helene giggled. "Yeah? Tell that to my mom. Or my sister. She keeps a paper bag in her purse for my really bad days."

"She puts a bag over your head?"

"Not mine—hers! She says she's too embarrassed to be seen with me." In fact, Alexis had only put the bag over her head once, as a joke, but she still carried it around in her purse. Whenever she pulled it out, the girls never failed to collapse in peals of laughter. "Anyway," Helene said, "it's just different now. Knowing that how I look is supposed to mean something to other people, and not just me."

Daniel nodded his head thoughtfully. He sipped his coffee before speaking. "Are you having second thoughts about working for Vedette?"

Helene warmed her hands with the cup, even though the weather was stiflingly hot. "Not second thoughts, exactly. I just wish I felt more passionately about it."

Daniel nodded his head. "And what do you feel passionate about?"

"Oh, all sorts of things," Helene said. Her eyes assumed a dreamy, faraway expression. "Art, music, history. The older I get, the more interests I develop. I used to think the reason I couldn't decide on a career was because I was flaky. But Lazlo doesn't think so. Lazlo says—" Helene cut herself short. Ix-nay on the Azlo-lay, stupid!

She took a deep breath and tried to regain her composure. She smiled and batted her eyelashes. "I can see why they call you the Prince of Paris. You have a way with women. Tell me, are you always so attentive to your models?"

Daniel put his coffee cup down and said, "Not always. You're very special to me, Helene. You've got a certain indefinable quality that I find fascinating."

Helene's throat grew thick. Was Daniel D'Artois flirting with her?

"I'm sorry I was so self-conscious today at the photo shoot. I'm a little nervous around you. I want so much to live up to your expectations of me. I'm just not used to this kind of attention."

"Well, I hope you do get used to it, because I believe you have tremendous potential as a model, provided you become less self-conscious. I have an idea. There is a designer at Vedette, who is just your age. She, too, takes work very seriously. I have asked her to help create a clothing line for young women, one that is more reflective of your own whimsical spirit. I would like very much for the two of you to meet."

Helene's couldn't believe what she was hearing. "This young designer . . . she wouldn't happen to be a beautiful American brunette, would she?"

Daniel looked startled. "How did you know?"

"Because she's my best friend. I mean, she's my sister. Well, really my stepsister." Helene drew a deep breath. "I guess I'm not really sure what our relationship is right now. It's sort of complicated."

Daniel leaned forward, his eyes sparkling. "Tell me. I love complications."

Helene told him the long story of her friendship with Alexis. How they had started out as stepsisters with seemingly nothing in common and had become best friends. She mentioned their mutual family troubles, as well as last summer's adventure in London, when they'd both competed for Prince William's affection.

By the time she filled him in on their latest fight, the sun was setting, smearing bands of purple, scarlet, and gold across the sky. "And even though we promised never to go after the same guy, here we are in Paris, doing exactly the same thing."

Daniel smiled. "And may I ask who the new objective is? He is a lucky man indeed."

Helene blushed to the roots of her hair. "I'm not at liberty to say. Oh, it's hopeless, anyway. Any man in his right mind would choose Alexis over me. Wouldn't you agree?" she asked cagily.

He covered her hand reassuringly. "*Courage,* Mademoiselle. Do not let the flames of jealousy engulf you. My interest in Mademoiselle Worth is purely professional."

It terrified her to say it, but she took strength in the fact that Daniel's hand still lingered over hers. "And your interest in me?"

Daniel paused a moment, as if considering his answer. "You know, I am glad to hear that a young girl like yourself is so well-read. And while I admire Monsieur Hemingway enormously, I prefer the works of another author who frequented Paris: Oscar Wilde."

Helene's eyes widened. "You mean you're . . .",

Daniel's eyes wandered over to the waiter, who was hovering nearby. He gave him a barely perceptible wink, then looked back at Helene. "Gay? Yes. But in France we are not as boisterous about declaring it as you are in the States. And my father, too, likes me to be discreet. For the sake of the business."

Helene wasn't sure what Daniel's sexual orientation

had to do with business, but the slightly harder edge to his voice warned her not to ask. Instead, she gave a wry laugh. "Too bad I didn't have my pet psychic with me. I could have saved myself a lot of trouble. Well, so much for my romantic summer in Paris."

Shaking his head, Daniel said, "I think you can salvage the trip by settling your differences with Alexis."

She squared her shoulders rebelliously. "After what she did to me? Sucking up to my evil witch of a stepmother, just for the sake of a lousy job? With friends like that, who needs enemies?"

Daniel reached out and put a placating hand on her arm. "It seems to me that you are being very uncharitable. I don't think Alexis accepted the internship to win favor with your stepmother. She has a genuine passion for design. I have seen it myself. It would be criminal to ask her to set it aside for the sake of pride."

Helene bowed her head with shame. "Maybe you're right. Still, Alexis *swore* no guy would ever get in the way of our friendship again. And now look what she's doing! How can I ever trust her again?"

Daniel said, "Ask yourself this: Do you really think Alexis came all the way to Paris for the sole purpose of stealing your love interest? Or did she have some other motive for coming?"

"She said she was coming to give me moral support,"

Helene admitted. "I was depressed about meeting my new stepmother."

Daniel threw up his hands in triumph. "*Voilà!* So sometime between Alexis's arrival and your quarrel, there was a misunderstanding. Her feelings were hurt. And so, instead of revealing her vulnerability, she lashed out at the very person she loves most in the world."

"You mean me?" Helene asked in a small voice.

Daniel nodded vigorously. "It is an old story. Let me ask you: Had your sister been the victim of betrayal recently?"

Helene thought back to Alexis's arrival in Paris, when she had acted so nonchalant about the cancelled Greek cruise. Vanessa's rejection *had* been a betrayal. And Helene had been so wrapped up in her own problems that she hadn't even thought about Alexis's pain. No wonder her sister had lashed out at her!

Ripping her paper napkin into small pieces, she said, "Yes, Lexy was betrayed. By her mother. And now by me. Oh, Daniel, I feel so awful. How am I ever going to make things right between us?"

"By offering a sincere apology. The sooner you do it, the better."

"It's not going to be easy. I think she stays late at work just so she won't have to see me when she gets home. I could station myself in her bedroom tonight and try to *make* her listen to me," Helene said doubtfully.

Daniel tapped his teeth thoughtfully, then said, "No, cornering her at your father's house will just make her feel more defensive. You have to meet on neutral ground." He snapped his fingers. "I have got it. Come to Vedette tomorrow at nine A.M. We're going to have a meeting about the new clothing line."

"And then?"

Daniel brandished his spoon as if waving a magical wand. "Leave the rest to your fairy godfather. The terrible spell that has been cast upon you is about to be broken."

Thirteen

Remembrance of Things Past

"What a fabulous movie. Thanks for taking me, Philippe; I really needed some cheering up," Alexis said. After work, they had caught a show around the corner from work, then walked to the Seine, where they boarded the Batobus at Trocadéro for the ride home. As with so many of her favorite pleasures in Paris, Philippe had introduced her to this marvelous water shuttle, which afforded fabulous glimpses of the city for a fraction of the cost of a guided tour. Alexis leaned against the rail and let the wind from the Seine ruffle her straight dark hair.

Philippe leaned beside her, wiping his eyeglasses clean. "I liked it, too, although I must say I was a little dismayed when you told me the title of your choice."

Alexis giggled. "*How to Marry a Millionaire*. Well, you must admit, it was educational."

"Are you really so interested in finding a rich husband?" Philippe asked wistfully. "It seems to me that a talented girl like you could make her own money and marry a man for love."

Her face hardened. "I used to think that myself, until I realized there is no such thing as love. Not really. No matter how much you trust a person, they always let you down in the end. You've got to look after your own interests in this world."

Philippe raised his eyebrows. "I thought you found the movie educational. If you had really been paying attention, you'd realize its message was completely opposite to what you just said."

Alexis shrugged. "Sort of. But if you noticed, Lauren Bacall ended up finding both money *and* happiness, all because she refused to marry a poor man."

Holding up a protesting hand, Philippe said, "Actually, she winds up leaving her rich fiancé for the man she loves, only to discover that her new boyfriend is actually loaded. It's just a happy coincidence that she winds up with a wealthy husband."

"Well, if you're going to get technical about it, I suppose you're right," Alexis admitted grudgingly. "Still, it was fun seeing it together. Helene would have never agreed to it."

"Helene?" Philippe frowned. Then his brow cleared. "Ah, yes, Helene. I've taken several photos of her for Daniel. I get the impression she doesn't enjoy the job too much, like she would rather feed the pigeons than pose for pictures."

"She must be loads of fun to work with," Alexis said sarcastically.

Philippe shrugged. "Models are seldom loads of fun to work with, and your sister, for her own reasons, is just as difficult as any. However, I do like photographing her. You never know what she's going to do next. I take it the two of you don't share many interests?"

Alexis snorted. "I'll say. If she does go to a movie, it's got to have social relevance. You know, one of those documentaries that makes you feel awful because we live in such a horrible world?"

He laughed. "Yes, I know the type. I, on the other hand, prefer films that take me *away* from real life, and transport me to a place of beauty."

"Exactly," she said eagerly. "Like those old Hollywood musicals, with the colorful costumes and sets. They always manage to inspire me, even when I'm in a rotten mood, like I was today."

"I noticed you were upset and had meant to ask why. It seems to me that everything is going your way. You've been given a plum assignment, and you're fast becoming the favorite designer of your boss. What more could you ask for?"

"I actually wasn't thinking about work at all. What's

really bothering me is Helene. We had a fight." Her voice trembled.

Philippe's gave her a look of concern. "About what?"

Alexis then told the whole, long story. How she and Helene had started out as stepsisters, then become best friends. How they'd competed for the same guy last summer. (She neglected to say it was Prince William.) How they'd decided never to behave as rivals ever again. Then all about their trip to Paris and their fight over Alexis's internship. And then how Helene had gotten the mistaken impression that Alexis was trying to woo Daniel D'Artois, whom Helene already had her sights set on. By the time Alexis finished the story, they were nearing their stop at the Louvre.

Philippe pushed his glasses up on his nose, a serious expression on his face. A cute little crease appeared between his eyebrows. He's a good listener, Alexis thought, grateful to finally unburden her problems on a sympathetic friend. Normally, Helene played that role. Ever since their fight, however, that outlet had been closed.

They disembarked and crossed the pont des Arts, walking in the direction of Chez Masterson. For a few minutes, they were both silent. Philippe seemed to be turning the story over in his mind.

"So what do you think?" Alexis finally asked. "Do you think Helene and I will ever be friends again?"

He placed his hand on the small of her back, firmly steering her past a group of teenagers who were muttering lewd remarks. Alexis felt a surge of gratitude. After they were a safe distance from the perverts, Philippe said, "I am reminded of an American movie that is close to my heart. It exactly encapsulates your situation."

"Really? What's it called?"

"*Dumb & Dumber.* Perhaps you have seen it?"

Alexis burst out laughing. "Yes, I'm familiar with that great work. Which one am I, the guy with the bowl haircut or the one with the explosive diarrhea?"

"Is there a difference?"

For a minute, Alexis was silent. She was looking toward the grand old church, but she wasn't really seeing it. Instead, she found herself thinking back on all the good times she and Helene had shared over the years. Like when Alexis got her first period, then kept it a secret from Helene for three months, not wanting her sister to feel underdeveloped. As it turned out Helene had gotten hers two weeks earlier, and had kept silent for the same reason.

The only reason they found out about the other's secret is that Helene went to get something from Alexis's purse and found a sanitary napkin inside. She had flung the evidence down on the school lunch table like a gauntlet, causing everybody to shriek and scatter in all differ-

ent directions. Everybody, that is, except Alexis. She just
giggled helplessly. Soon, Helene joined in, and by the
time the cafeteria monitor came over, the two of them
were doubled over, clutching their stomachs and howling
with laughter.

Seeing her wistful smile, Philippe asked, "What are
you thinking?"

"I was thinking about something I read a long time
ago. About the nature of relationships. The Buddha
believed whenever a person enters your life, you should
welcome them and enjoy whatever it is they bring, even
it it's only for a short time. Then, when it's time for them
to go away, you shouldn't take it as a rejection, because
when a person leaves your life, it has nothing to do with
you. It's simply time for them to leave. Do you believe
that?" Her voice was tentative, not at all self-assured like
it normally was.

So maybe this was the difference between French boys
and American boys. When Alexis said, "The Buddha
believes . . . ," Philippe didn't laugh or say "The who?" or
"Didn't Keanu Reeves play him in a movie?" or "Did he
rap on the last D12 album?" Instead he said, "I think the
Buddha's example takes a rather one-sided view of relationships. For instance, there's a difference between when
a person voluntarily leaves your life, and when a person
has been deliberately driven away."

Alexis started sniffling. "You're right. I know it. Helene didn't turn her back on me. She withdrew after I accused her of being a lousy friend. Really, I was just taking out my anger on her for other stuff. Oh, Philippe, how am I ever going to make it up to her?" Looking up, Alexis saw that they had reached the Masterson home. "I'm not ready to go inside yet. Can we take another walk around the block?"

"Of course," Philippe said. "But you must remember that French blocks aren't square like American ones. You never know where a turn around the corner might take us."

Alexis was too wrapped in her own thoughts to hear the new tone in Philippe's voice. Instead, she said, "I just don't know what to do. I've messed everything up, haven't I?"

"Nonsense. It takes two obstinate stepsisters to make one catfight. If Helene is half as independent—"

"Half?" Alexis cut him off. "She's twice as independent as me! Ten times as independent!"

Philippe laughed. "Yes, I can believe that after today. Nevertheless, it's obvious what you must do."

Alexis grabbed his hand and pulled them to a stop. "What? Tell me, Philippe."

"You must be the bigger person and apologize. And soon, before your sister's wounds begin to fester."

"But how? We're not even on speaking terms. Every

time I walk past her bedroom, the door is shut and the light is off. I think she purposely goes to sleep before I get home, just so she won't have to talk to me."

"And you work late, so that you'll miss her."

Alexis nodded sheepishly. An empty office was still better than the awkwardness at home.

Philippe seemed lost in thought. He pursed his lips, and Alexis found herself noticing them. It was a totally inappropriate moment to do so, but she found herself thinking that kissing Philippe would be a lot nicer than trying to find a solution to her Helene problem.

But before she could do anything rash, Philippe snapped his fingers. "I've got it! Didn't Daniel say he wanted you to meet with Helene, to discuss the dress you're supposed to design for her?"

She squeezed his arm excitedly. "Yeah! He said I needed to get a feel for her personality so I could design something that would reflect Vedette's new sensibility. I, um, I didn't mention that we were sisters."

"Well, all you have to do is get Daniel to arrange the meeting. That way, Helene will *have* to speak to you." Philippe slowed his pace as the Masterson home came into view again.

Impulsively, Alexis jumped to kiss his cheek. "Philippe, it's perfect! I'll work out everything I have to say tonight, before going to sleep."

Philippe grinned, then put a warning hand on her arm. "Don't prepare *too* much. Your apology should sound sincere." He stopped walking just before they reached the front door. "Besides, you're never more charming than when you speak from the heart."

Alexis's face flushed. "Thanks, Philippe. I'll definitely follow your advice." She paused, as if trying to find the right words. Finally, she continued. "You know, I really appreciate all you've done for me this summer. If it hadn't been for you, this whole trip would have been a complete disaster."

Philippe arched his right eyebrow. "Even with the internship?"

"Even with the internship. I'm starting to realize that having a great job is all well and good, but it's not really a substitute for companionship." She looked up, confused. "I mean, friendship. I mean . . . well, I guess you know what I mean."

For a second, she thought he was going to kiss her. Then, just at the critical moment, he took a step backward. "It's getting late, and I've got a long day ahead of me tomorrow. I'd better be going home." He tugged at the collar of his shirt, then abruptly turned in the direction of the métro.

Alexis stared after him. There's a difference between when a person voluntarily leaves your life, and when a person has been deliberately driven away. She turned around and went to unlock the front door. The lock was stiff and old, and it was a struggle to use the key. "Well, I can hardly be accused of driving him away. After all, I made it clear from the very first that I'm not interested in dating poor students," she muttered. "Anyway, what do I care what he thinks? I'm just interested in making up with Helene now." She threw her entire weight against the door, and it finally gave way with a protesting groan.

Fourteen

The Spell Is Broken

Padding softly to her room, Alexis saw a light shining beneath Helene's door. I'm sick of all this tiptoeing around, she thought. She pushed gently at the door and peeked inside.

Helene, inspired by her conversation with Daniel, was trying out poses in front of a full-length mirror. Unfortunately, she still wasn't sure how one "acted natural." Even imaging Philippe with his camera made her feel stiff and strange. For example, what do you do with your hands when you're not actually using them? Helene's just seemed to hang off her arms like fish on poles. And one's feet? Were they both supposed to face forward? Or did you turn one out to the side so that you looked like, hey, I'm just standing here. Camera? What camera? Helene tried to remember how she would stand when she was just hanging around, but it wasn't the sort of thing she'd ever paid attention to. In the end, she got so frustrated that she imagined there were strings tied to her wrists and ankles and head, and she was just getting into a rendition of the marionette's dance from *The Sound of Music* when a giggle sounded behind her. As she whirled around, Alexis pushed the door open.

"What are you *doing*?" Alexis managed to sputter out between laughs.

"Acting natural," Helene stammered. "Daniel said I need to practice."

"Sure, 'natural,'" Alexis said, exaggerating Helene's jerky movements. "Natural if you're Pinocchio."

"I'm sorry," Helene said, laughing. "That looks like The Robot, and I was doing the puppet scene from *The Sound of Music*."

"*The Sound of Music*?" Alexis squealed. "Funky Chicken is more like it."

Helene threw a pillow and at her sister. "Or Not-So-Funky Chicken, in your case." She flopped down on the bed. "Oh, my God," she said. "Are we getting along?"

Alexis, still carrying the pillow, bent down on one knee and held it out to Helene. "My Queen, I come bearing the Royal Pillow of Apology. Please accept it with my most sincere request for your forgiveness for being a royal pain in the butt."

Helene sat up and took the pillow from Alexis.

"Your Queen accepts the Royal Pillow, and now exercises her right to—" She finished her sentence by whomping Alexis in the head, then handed the pillow to her sister. "You may now take your free shot."

Alexis whomped. The two girls' hair looked like a pair of mismatched birds' nests.

"*Dumb & Dumber,*" Alexis murmured.

"Which one am I . . . the one with diarrhea?" Helene demanded.

"No, the one with the stupid haircut."

Helene pointed at Alexis's disheveled head. "Um, I think you're giving me a run for my money in that competition." The two of them started laughing.

They sighed and sank down on the bed. "Just for the record," Helene said. "I was going to apologize to you tomorrow morning. Daniel is calling a meeting to discuss the new fashion line, and I thought it would be the perfect opportunity to tell you what a jerk I've been."

Alexis shook her head. "No, I'm the one who's been a jerk. First of all, I should have never let Margot come between us like that. I knew she offered me the internship just to get back at you. But I was so excited, I didn't even think about how it would affect you." She looked down at her hands. "And then that whole business about going after Daniel—I promise you I was never trying to do that. It was just a misunderstanding. Can you ever forgive me?"

"Don't be an idiot. I should have never discouraged

you from taking the internship, knowing how much it meant to you. Daniel tells me you're doing a great job," Helene said.

Alexis gave a weak smile. "Well, I've been being very nice to him, with the intention of eventually turning him in the direction of my beautiful sister."

Helene smiled a little smile, knowing she knew something Alexis didn't. "Nope. He's being totally sincere about your talent."

"How can you be sure? Has he been flirting with you? Maybe you didn't even need my help!"

Helene grabbed the Royal Pillow of Apology and buried her face in it to stifle her shrieking laughter—no sense drawing attention from Margot or Mr. Masterson. "Believe me, Alexis," she said when she could talk again, "I am not even *remotely* his type."

"Well," Alexis said huffily, "what exactly *is* his type, then? My sister is hardly chopped liver, you know."

"Oh, I think he's looking for somebody more, um, what's the word I'm looking for?" Helene drew out the suspense so long, Alexis threatened her with the much-abused pillow. "The Prince of Paris isn't looking for a princess," she said finally. "More like a page. Or a duke. Or maybe even a buff vassal." Helene could barely suppress her giggles.

Alexis's eyes widened. "Daniel D'Artois is gay!?!"

Helene shushed her. "Tell the whole city, why don't you?" Then, in a more normal voice, she said, "Yeah, I totally made my move this afternoon, and he confided in me. I guess the family keeps it kind of quiet because they're in the public eye." She sighed. "It certainly doesn't look like I'm going to find a hot new boyfriend on this trip. I guess I'll just have to settle for being a world-famous model."

Alexis pouted and spoke in a mock-baby voice: "Oh, poor Helene." But then she grabbed her sister's hand. "Actually, I think I have the perfect guy for you. He's not exactly an heir—"

"Or an heiress," Helen threw in, and giggled.

"—but he is awfully nice," Alexis finished, smirking. "And C-U-T-E cute."

Helene sat up and started braiding Alexis's hair. "If he's so N-I-C-E and C-U-T-E, why don't you go out with him your S-E-L-F?"

"Okay, first of all," Alexis said. "The spelling thing? A bad move on my part. Let's abandon it before this conversation drags on for T-W-O more hours. As for Philippe, well, he's just a poor film student, and I'm looking for someone who can keep me in style." Grateful she didn't have to look her sister in the eye, Alexis went on, "He is *totally* cute and funny, and I know you'd like him a lot. Like, he has a safety pin holding on one of the arms of his glasses. That's so Helene, right? Not Alexis."

"I don't know whether I should be pleased or offended that you associate me with broken things," Helene said, giving a fake pull on Alexis's hair. "Philippe, huh? *C'est francais, ooh-la-la!*"

Alexis didn't correct her sister's horrible pronunciation. "Actually, I think you already know him. Philippe Martin, the photography intern from Vedette. He says he's done a couple of photo shoots with you."

Helene stopped braiding. "*That* Philippe! Ooh-la-la," she said again. "He *is* cute. But what makes you think he'd want to go out on a date with me?"

"Well, in the first place, you're Helene Masterson. Fabulous, funky, fearless—not to mention the new face of Vedette. And then, you know, he already told me he found you very interesting. Actually, I feel kind of bad for him. For the past couple of weeks he's gone out of his way to take me around town. It's probably been hell for him. I can see him cringe whenever I miss one of his historical allusions."

"Lex, don't put yourself down. You're Alexis Worth, beautiful, bold, brash, and designing the dress that will take Vedette into the twenty-first century. If he doesn't like you, he's nuts."

Alexis thought of her good-bye with Philippe, then shook

her head. "I don't know. Sometimes I think maybe there's a spark, but then other times it feels like he hangs out with me just because we both put in such long hours. We're usually the last ones at the office. He's got a good excuse: He's working his way through school and needs the extra money. But I was just there because I didn't know where else to go. It felt so awful coming home, knowing you hated my guts."

Helene's eyes welled up. "I didn't hate your guts. I was jealous of all the success you were having in Paris. I've always felt like a bit of a chump next to you. You're so sleek and smooth and sophisticated. Lazlo would have never stopped writing you if you'd gotten together."

Alexis looked her at sister quizzically.

"Lazlo?"

"What?" Helene said, looking away. "Slip of the tongue. I meant Simon."

Alexis grabbed Helene's hand. "Are you pining away for your British boy?"

"Don't be silly," Helene said. "He can't even be bothered to write me." She tried to get up, but Alexis held her down.

"Helene, Lazlo was totally head over heels in love with you. Remember when we were leaving that pub and I found that book he had left behind? And how he said, 'Thanks, Simon,' when I handed it to him, because he was so busy staring at you?"

Helene sniffed. "If I'm so great, how come I haven't heard a word from him since May?"

"Because he's a loser." Alexis sighed. "L-O-S-E-R loser. As in, he lost you, and it's his loss. I'm tired of watching you waste your energy on twits like Lazlo and Jeremy. It's about time you went out and dated some other guys. Remember, you've got to kiss a lot of frogs before you finally meet Prince Charming."

Rubbing her eyes, Helene mumbled, "I guess so. Maybe my date with Philippe will be so great that I'll finally forget the little jerk."

At the thought of Philippe and Helene sitting at the kind of noisy sidewalk café he had taken her to, Alexis's heart contracted for some reason. "I hope so, honey. Well, there's no point in us sitting up talking all night. We've got an early morning ahead of us. Daniel is determined to make this new clothing line the toast of the town."

Helene tried to strike a "natural" pose, then sighed wearily. "I only hope I'm up to it."

"Don't worry, Helene," Alexis said, rubbing her best friend's shoulder. "The MasterWorth team is back in action. Nothing can stop us now." The sisters shared a long, heartfelt hug, and then Alexis went to her bedroom and fell into bed.

• • •

The next day, Helene and Alexis walked arm and arm into Vedette. At the sight of his two hand-picked protégées whispering and giggling together, Daniel broke into a huge smile.

"I'm glad you girls have put your differences behind you. The fall fashion show is just around the corner. All the designers are working around the clock to create clothes that will reflect Vedette's new young, hip sensibility. Instead of hiring models, I'm going to be using famous young actresses: Lindsay Lohan. Brittany Murphy. Katie Holmes. Mary-Kate and Ashley Olsen. Alexis, you'll be designing the piece that will set the tone for the whole collection: a white ball gown fit for a rock-and-roll queen. Helene will come out wearing it at the very end of the show, to a fanfare of trumpets. Does this appeal to you both?"

"Oh, yes, Daniel!" Alexis exclaimed, her eyes sparkling like sapphires.

"Uh, I guess so," quavered Helene. "I mean, how many people are going to be at this show, anyway?"

Daniel leaned forward, concerned. "*Chérie,* I would not ask you to do this show if I did not feel you were up to it. I have asked Philippe to spend the whole day with you, to get you acclimated. Everything will be fine. I promise."

Helene nodded uncertainly.

Daniel laughed. "I can see you can barely contain your enthusiasm. Well, let's not waste any more time talking about the big day. We must start preparing for it." He leaned to speak into the intercom. "Janine? Please ask Philippe Martin to come to my office."

Moments later, the door opened and Philippe walked in. He was wearing a cobalt blue workshirt that exactly matched the color of his eyes. If he couldn't take Helene's mind off Lazlo, Alexis didn't know who could. She noticed then that Philippe had fixed his glasses: The safety pin was gone. He kept fiddling with the repaired hinge, and it seemed to Alexis that he used his hand to cast side-long glances her way. Her heart fluttered.

"Philippe," Daniel said then, "I believe you know Mademoiselles Worth and Masterson. I am giving you the enviable task of molding Mademoiselle Helene into the new face of Vedette. Does this assignment appeal to you?"

Philippe grinned good-naturedly. "I've had worse."

"*Bon!* I will send Mademoiselle Alexis to the design studio, where she will create a ravishing new gown. And now, if you will excuse me, I have a few phone calls to make. Those Olsen twins have been particularly elusive, and I am determined to have them in my show." With a wave of his hand, Daniel dismissed them all.

The three drifted over to the coffeemaker in the

waiting room of Daniel's office. Turning to Philippe, Alexis said brightly, "Since you and Helene are going to be working so closely together, I thought you might want to get dinner together or something. I think if you got to know each other, Helene might be able to relax more in front of the camera. And I think you'll find you have *a lot* in common."

Helene turned brick red. She had expected Alexis to set her up on a date with Philippe, but not this way! "Oh, Lexy, don't be silly. I'm sure Philippe will be sick of me after working with me all day."

Philippe, meanwhile, was looking at Alexis funny, but she refused to meet his gaze. "It would be my pleasure to share a meal with you," he said finally, turning to Helene. "Are you free tomorrow evening?"

Helene sensed the tension between Philippe and Alexis, and smiled her brightest smile to try to cover it up. "Sure! Why don't you come by and pick me up around seven o'clock? Maybe we could go to a movie, or something."

Philippe's eyes shone with excitement. "I know the perfect one. Only, would it be all right if I picked you up at six thirty?"

"Great. Well, we'd better get down to work. I don't want Daniel to think we're slacking off." Helene turned to her sister, "I'll see you at dinner tonight, okay?"

"I hope so. But, um"—Alexis glanced at Philippe, then down at the floor—"I might have to work late, though."

"Well, stop by my room before you go to bed, anyway. I want to hear all about the dress you're designing," Helene told her. Then, turning to Philippe, she asked, "Shall we?" and hooked her arm through his. She smiled at Alexis over her shoulder as they walked toward the photography studio together.

Alexis watched them disappear around the corner. She had a smile plastered on her face, but as hard as she tried, she couldn't manage to feel happy.

Fifteen

Some Like It Not

The next night, Philippe came by punctually at 6:30 to pick Helene up for their date. He paled a little when she came to the door wearing a zebra-striped camisole and a leopard-spotted miniskirt.

Seeing his reaction, Helene gave a good-natured laugh. "Every woman has her own particular fashion icon. Alexis patterns her look after Audrey Hepburn; I pattern mine after Wilma Flintstone."

Philippe smiled shyly and extended a single red rose. "I thought you might like this."

"Hey, thanks!" Helene said, taking the rose and twirling it between her fingers. "It's just beautiful." I can see why Alexis was gushing about this guy, Helene thought. She's always been a sucker for flowers. Realizing they were standing in the doorway, she stepped into the hall and invited him inside. "Please, come in. I'd like you to meet my family."

Mr. Masterson, Margot, and Alexis were sitting in the

green and white salon. Mr. Masterson was seated in front of his laptop, muttering under his breath as he always did when he was working. Margot was stretched out on the chaise longue sipping white wine, and Alexis was painting her nails in the corner with an air of nonchalance. From her stiff posture, though, Helene knew she was tense about something. Poor kid, she thought affectionately. She thinks I'm still hung up on Lazlo, and worries I'll make a mess of the date. Silly thing.

"Dad, Margot, I'd like you to meet Philippe Martin." Helene's voice sounded sweet and syrupy, like it always did when she was talking to authority figures. "He's taking me to the movies tonight."

Mr. Masterson looked up suspiciously. "Just how long have you known my daughter, and where are you taking her?"

Philippe adjusted his glasses. "I'm a photographer at Vedette, sir. Helene and I know each other from work. I thought we'd go to the Cinéma en Plein Air tonight. There's a very good picture there."

Helene's dad gave a dissatisfied grunt. "A fashion photographer, huh? It must be hard work, gazing at beautiful girls all day. Just remember, when it comes to my daughter, looking is one thing. Touching is a whole different story."

Helene had never seen Mr. Masterson do the

overprotective-father thing, and she had to work hard to keep a straight face.

"Well, uh, it's getting late," she said brightly. "We'd better be going." She grabbed Philippe's arm, spun him around, and pushed him out of the salon. "We'll probably go out to dinner after the movie, so don't wait up!" she yelled over her shoulder.

They walked out the front door, and Helene sagged into an exhausted heap on the top step. Her eyes were crossed and her tongue was lolling out. Philippe laughed. A few seconds later, Alexis slipped out to join them.

Seeing Helene slumped on the step, Alexis started giggling. "Wow, I didn't know Trevor had the whole caveman thing in him," she said.

Helene smacked herself in the head. "So *that's* where I got my Wilma Flintstone obsession from."

"Does this mean you'd like a gravel engagement ring?" asked Philippe.

"Why not choose something more classic, like a bone?" Alexis snapped. "Listen, you two. Helene's dad is about to have a stroke in there. He can't stand the thought of his precious baby going out on a date with a Frenchman."

Philippe shrugged. "So what can she do? Nothing she says will change her father's mind. He is obviously irrational." Helene nodded in agreement.

"What I suggest," Alexis offered, "is that you bring Helene home early, right after the movie. That way, you'll gain Mr. Masterson's trust."

Helene burst out laughing. "Oh come on, Lex, I think that was mostly for show. In fact, I think Dad's just displacing a little of his anxiety about the way men are always fawning over Margot onto me."

"Well, all the same," Alexis said, "it can't hurt to come home early tonight. Actually," she went on, "I think it's sweet that your dad is so worried. No offense," she added hastily when Philippe opened his mouth to protest.

Helene gave her sister an affectionate hug. "Alexis, you're weird. But that's why I love you. Don't worry about us. We're sure to have a good time once we escape this lunatic asylum."

Philippe lingered at the top of the steps, where Alexis stood with her arms crossed. "Have a good night," he said finally.

"Yeah, have fun yourselves," Alexis said sourly. Then, just as they were almost out of earshot, she yelled, "Don't do anything I wouldn't do!" They waved vaguely in response.

It turned out that the Cinéma en Plein Air wasn't a movie house; it was actually an outdoor film festival held in a park. A huge screen set up on an expansive green lawn, and people brought lawn chairs and picnic baskets. Children and dogs ran riot everywhere, in contrast to the romantic couples settled down on blankets. Everywhere you looked there seemed to be a pair of lovers cuddling and kissing, oblivious to the hubbub around them.

The festive French spirit that Helene loved so much was in full force, yet somehow she couldn't manage to enter into it. For one thing, it was an awfully hot evening—she could feel her eye liner melting off through the entire movie. For another, the film was a bit of a snooze-fest: *West Side Story*. She'd seen it years ago when she was a little kid and had thought it was corny even then. When the gang members burst into song, she turned to make a sarcastic joke to Philippe. To her total astonishment, Philippe seemed to be *enjoying* the movie! He actually burst into applause at the end of certain numbers, as did many of the surrounding audience members. Helene shook her head. Amazing what some people consider entertaining, she thought.

Finally, the picture ended and everybody started gathering their stuff together to go home. Helene struggled to her feet, which wasn't easy since she was wearing three-inch platforms. Philippe leaned to help her, but she waved him away. "No, thanks, I'm fine. Serves me right for wearing heels to a park!"

Philippe frowned with concern. "I'm sorry, I should have told you the film was outdoors. I thought it would be a fun surprise."

"Oh, it *was,*" Helene assured him, not too convincingly. "I just wish the movie had been a little shorter."

"You didn't like it?!" Philippe asked, amazed. "I thought everybody loved *West Side Story*!"

"I guess Alexis didn't tell you, but I'm more into movies with gritty realism. Like *Mean Streets.*"

"Come to think of it, Alexis did say you liked those sorts of movies," he admitted. "But I didn't think your dislike of fantasy included *West Side Story.*"

"It's just that it's all so unbelievable," Helene said bluntly as they finally reached avenue Jean Jaurès. "All that singing and dancing. A real turf war would have been a bloody mess."

Philippe pleaded the movie's case. "Both Tony and Bernardo got stabbed to death, and Anita almost got raped."

"And they never stopped singing the whole time," Helene scoffed. "Not exactly cinema verité," she added in a voice that, even to her ears, sounded a little too harsh. Seeing Philippe's look of dismay, she grinned. "Sorry. I guess I'm a bit of a ghoul. It's like with this trip. I've always been interested in the gory parts of French history. The storming of the Bastille. The Reign of Terror. Robespierre and the Black Death. You know, the fun stuff."

Philippe gave a mock shudder.

They reached the métro and pounded down the stairs. A train pulled in just as they went through the turnstiles, and they boarded the nearest car.

"Don't worry. I realize I'm not the typical tourist," Helene said as she sank gratefully into a vacant seat. The air conditioning felt blissfully cool after the stifling heat of the park. "When I was in London last year, I took a walking tour of Jack the Ripper's favorite haunts and thought it was phenomenal." Her face glowed at the memory.

Philippe laughed. "I prefer to get up early and watch the fog lift over the Thames."

She turned to regard him quizzically. "You're a romantic, like Alexis. She adores all that glossy, glamorized stuff. When she came to Paris, all she wanted to do was gaze at the moon from the top of the Eiffel Tower and go on picnics at Versailles." Helene sighed, shaking her head as if she couldn't understand such strange tastes. "Ah, well, I guess it's normal." She ducked to avoid a woman wielding a large shoulder bag and added, "She sure wasn't acting very normal tonight, though. What was all that business about us getting home early? And why was she was so concerned about Dad's reaction all of the sudden?"

Philippe looked depressed. "Maybe she agrees with him and thinks I am a predatory Frenchman."

"*That* can't be it. Otherwise, why would she go to the trouble of setting us up? "You should have heard her talking about you last night. She went on and on about how smart and funny and romantic you are. It was almost as if . . ."

"As if what?" Philippe prompted.

Helene put her hands up to her mouth, horrified. "Oh, no. I was going to say, it was almost as if she was in love with you."

Philippe looked at her with stricken eyes. "What are you saying?"

"I'm saying she likes you, stupid! That's why she was so uptight about our going out together."

He shook his head in disbelief. "If she was interested, it doesn't make sense that she would try to set us up." His shoulders sagged. "She'd never go out with me. I'm only a poor student."

Seeing his look of dejection, Helene clapped her hands delightedly. "Oh, my God, you like her, too! This is PER-FECT!" she shrieked. Now everybody on the train was looking at them. Luckily, they were just approaching Gare de l'Est, where they were supposed to transfer to the 4 train. She dragged Philippe to his feet and pulled him out of the car with her.

"Helene, you're being absurd," he protested as they bobbed and weaved through the crowd on the way to the other train. "There is no way your sister shares my feelings. Her behavior says everything to the contrary."

"That's just because you don't understand Alexis the way I do," Helene said confidently. As if by magic, the other train pulled up just as they reached the platform. They scrambled onboard, but this time there were no empty seats. Swinging from a strap handle, Helene continued, "My sister is kind of weird when it comes to relationships. It's not her fault, really. She didn't have a lot of stability growing up." She told Philippe how Vanessa had invited Alexis to spend the summer with her, only to cancel at the last minute. "Ever since then, she's been pretending that all she's after is a rich husband, but I don't buy it. I think she's afraid to admit what she really wants."

"And what is it she really wants?" Philippe asked, trying to steady himself as the train made several sharp turns.

"You, dummy," Helene said, swaying with the movement of the car. "Last night, when I complained about my lousy love life, she suggested I go out with you because you're so cultured and refined and magnificent."

Philippe turned red. "So if I'm so magnificent, why isn't she able to overlook the fact that I haven't got any money?"

"Look, Philippe, not to get all American and common, but neither Alexis nor I need to marry for money. Alexis's dad is one of the top PR guys in New York. Not only is she the only girl in our high school who's had dinner with Leonardo DiCaprio, she's had lunch with him too! She's just using that gold-digging act as a smokescreen." Helene paused for breath. "Believe me, she's afraid you'd reject her, or that you would think she's shallow."

He shook his head, as if in a daze. "I could never think that Alexis was shallow. She's the most beautiful, sensitive girl I know. Last week I took her to see *The Umbrellas of Cherbourg*. Afterward, she turned to me and said it had been like drinking champagne with her eyes. I've never met anybody with a gift for description like hers."

"Yeah, she's right up there with Proust," Helene said acidly. "Look, Valentino, now that you know the score, why don't you sweep her into your arms and declare yourself?" The train pulled into the St-Germain-des-Prés station, and they got off.

Exiting the turnstiles, Philippe said thoughtfully, "I'd love to, but I'm sure she would shoot me down. Like you said, Alexis isn't exactly normal when it comes to relationships."

Climbing the station steps, Helene answered him. "You're right. We'll have to develop a game plan." She reached the street. For a second, she lost sight of Philippe in the crowd of people pouring out of the station. Catching sight of him again, Helene snapped her fingers. "I've got it!" she crowed.

"You've got what?" Philippe asked confusedly, adjusting his glasses.

"The strategy for winning Alexis's heart," Helene said impatiently. "You guys have been virtually inseparable since the day you met, right?"

"Yes."

"So why not put a little distance between you?" Helene said. "Stop hanging around Alexis, propping up her ego. She needs to realize her true feelings for you, and that's only going to happen if you're not there to give her a daily Philippe fix."

They reached the rue du Four, where they were held fast by a traffic light. "How long should I avoid her?" Philippe asked.

"I'll tell you when to make your move," Helene assured him. "In the meantime, I think I'll get Daniel involved in this little scheme. Once Alexis starts missing you, she might get it into her head to arrange an accidental meeting at work. I'll ask Daniel to keep you guys apart from now until the fashion show. By that time, she'll be frantic to see you." The traffic light turned green. She raced across the street.

Struggling to keep up with her, Philippe said, "Helene, are you sure this is really going to work?"

"Leave it to me," she reassured him. "If you let me direct this picture, I can guarantee that it has a Hollywood finish."

Sixteen

Oui, Je Regrette Tous

When Helene got home from her date with Philippe, her father was sitting in the kitchen nursing a mug of hot milk. Helene bent to kiss him. "Hi, Daddy. Your ulcer acting up?" Her voice was deep with concern.

Mr. Masterson winced. "Yeah, my stomach had been doing pretty good for the past few months, then all of the sudden it flared up again." He took a sip of milk, then grimaced. "Right around Margot's movie premiere."

Helene leaned against the refrigerator. "I guess that *was* a pretty rough night for you, wasn't it?"

Mr. Masterson shrugged. "Margot seemed to take it in stride. I, on the other hand, still haven't gotten over it. Call me old-fashioned, but I can't get really get comfortable watching some young stud making love to my wife on-screen."

Seeing the pain on her father's face, she said gently, "Look, Daddy, I know seeing the movie was hard. But you have to remember, Margot's an *actress*. It's her job to kiss other guys and stuff. You must have known that when you married her."

"Yeah, well, she didn't have to be so enthusiastic about it," he barked. Realizing he was shouting, Mr. Masterson lowered his voice. "Helene, you're too young to understand, but marriage isn't dating. The whole point is to commit yourself wholly to a person, not to jump in and out of bed with everyone you meet."

"Which I *believe* was the point of Margot's movie," Helene said, her voice dripping with sarcasm. "Dad, I may be seventeen, but contrary to what you think, I do understand the seriousness of marriage. After all, I'm a child of divorce. *You're* the one who's on his second marriage, not me." Mr. Masterson started to interrupt angrily, but Helene raised her voice and finished what she had to say. "Furthermore, you're behaving as though Margot cheated on you, when she was actually just playing a part. Give me a break!"

Mr. Masterson opened his mouth as if he were about to respond, but instead, only got up from the table and left the room. A moment later, Helene felt a comforting arm being slipped around her shoulder. Startled, she turned to see Margot, who was standing beside her. Her stepmother was wearing a strange expression, as though she was on the verge of saying something but didn't know quite where to begin. Finally, Margot leaned forward and drew her into a hug. And a few moments, after recovering from her initial shock, Helene was actually able to hug back.

Hearing the clatter of pots and pans in the kitchen, Alexis got up to investigate. She got the shock of her life when she saw what had caused it. Sitting at the counter were Margot and Helene. From the dark mustache on Helene's upper lip, they appeared to be drinking hot chocolate. "What's all this?" Alexis demanded. "I thought you two were mortal enemies."

Margot smiled. "Peace has been declared, and we were celebrating over chocolate. Would you care for some?"

Alexis sat down next to Helene. "Sure, if I can have some whipped cream on mine."

Helene watched enviously as Margot spooned some whipped cream onto her sister's drink. "I shouldn't even be drinking this hot chocolate, with the big fashion show coming up. If Daniel saw me now, he'd have a fit."

"Yeah, for such a handsome guy, he sure is a slave driver," Alexis agreed.

"Don't be too hard on Daniel," Margot admonished. "He has a great deal of pressure on him trying to prove to his father that he can, indeed, take over Vedette."

Helene looked at Margot curiously. "How do you know so much about Daniel's problems, Margot?"

Her stepmother took a long sip of chocolate, then said, "Alain has been my friend for many years, ever since I first became an actress. He told me in the strictest confidence that he is worried about the future of the company, especially since Daniel will not produce an heir."

Helene shook her head. "But what can Monsieur D'Artois do about it? I mean, it would be the same thing if Daniel were straight and couldn't have any children."

"You must remember, Alain D'Artois is an old-fashioned man," Margot said. "For him, family is comprised of a husband, a wife, and many children. The fact that his son is unwilling to follow this pattern is a great source of heartache to him."

Alexis snorted. "Families. I think *they're* the source of all life's misery."

"Don't be so quick to condemn families, *chérie,*" said Margot. "I know that it is not easy being young in this day and age. My own parents were divorced when I was very small. Growing up, I vowed never to repeat their mistakes. Yet, within months of getting married, I cast myself in the role of the wicked stepmother."

Helene looked at her with frank curiosity. "Why, Margot? I mean, what was the point of being so nasty to me?"

Margot rose and took her empty cup to the sink, then spoke without turning around. "When I met your father,

I experienced a love that I had felt only once before. Before
my parents divorced, I was ... how do you say ... the apple
of my father's eye. Then, when he left my mother, things
changed. Each time we met, he seemed to be filled with
criticism. He didn't like the way I dressed, the way I wore
my hair, the way I spoke. The older I got, the worse our
relationship became."

It's just like Daniel said, Helene thought. Some fathers
really must have a hard time watching their daughters
grow up.

Margot continued: "The final straw was when I
decided to become an actress. My father told me I was
wasting my life. I became so angry, I told him I'd never
speak to him again. Three months later, he died."

Helene moved to put her hand on Margot's shoulder,
but her stepmother pulled away, as if she was embarrassed.

"Please, do not feel sorry for me. I am only trying to
explain why I behaved so terribly toward you, Helene.
You see, when I met Trevor, I had a second taste of
unconditional love. No matter what I did or how I
behaved, Trevor thought it was wonderful."

Helene's mind reached back to a tap dance recital long
ago. She must have been six. At the last minute, she had
refused to go on. Miss Sullivan, her dance instructor, had
yelled and called her a spoiled brat. At that moment, her

father had come backstage to investigate why Helene hadn't made her big appearance. Hearing the angry words being hurled at his daughter, Mr. Masterson stormed over and stepped between teacher and student. "Don't you *ever* speak to my child like that again," he said, getting within inches of Miss Sullivan's face. With that, he took Helene gently by the hand and guided her out to the car. They then drove out to her favorite ice-cream parlor, where he ordered double hot fudge sundaes for them both.

"So, when your father asked me to marry him, I accepted with great happiness. Once again, I was the apple of someone's eye. Only there was a small problem," Margot said.

"What was that?" Helene asked.

"Can't you guess?" her stepmother asked, smiling bitterly. "It was you!"

"Me?!" Helene gasped incredulously. "What have I got to do with this?"

"Even though your father said he loved me with all his heart, I always sensed a sadness in him. And it was a sadness I could not lift, no matter how hard I tried. At first, I thought it was because of the difference in our ages. A young girlfriend makes a man feel strong, powerful, attractive. A young wife makes him feel old, self-conscious, and a little bit silly." Margot sounded as if she, herself, were a hundred years old. "Finally, I came out and asked what was wrong. After insisting that everything was perfect, that his life couldn't be better, he finally admitted that he missed you."

"Well, he sure kept it a secret from Helene!" Alexis exploded. "Do you know how many times they've seen each other since the divorce? You could probably count the visits on one hand."

"Don't be unfair, Alexis," Helene said softly. "It's been eight times."

Margot looked at Helene beseechingly. "I know he should have made a greater effort to see you. But he seems to think that, after the divorce, you had no use for him. You were always praising your stepfather and how happy you were in your new home."

"Because I didn't want him to worry about me!" Helene burst out. "I didn't want to be like the other kids in school, dragged off to therapy the minute the divorce papers got signed. I wanted to prove I was adjusting well, so we could all get on with our lives."

Margot nodded slowly. "Yes, it makes sense. But your father was hurt. Always he tells me about how smart you are, and then goes on to say that he can't take credit for any of it, because he had no part in your upbringing."

"What a holy mess," Alexis protested. "Her dad loves Helene, but he won't go see her. Then, when she comes to see him, he's got nothing but criticism for her. My mother can't stand the sight of me, yet invites me to spend the summer with her on a cruise ship only to cancel at the last minute, because she suddenly realized what a bore parenting can be. I tell you, sometimes I think we would be better off being raised by wolves."

Helene and Margot burst out laughing. "Possibly," Margot admitted. "But then you'd miss all the fun of rebelling."

"According to the Buddha, rebellion is a manifestation of craving," Alexis said. "When we fully accept the reality of our situations, craving ceases, and with that, suffering. So I'm going to stop rebelling against the idea that my mother hates my guts, and just accept it. Once I stop craving her love, my suffering will cease."

"And then what will happen?" Helene asked.

"I will have achieved inner peace," Alexis said placidly. "Or at least avoid another stress-related acne breakout."

Suddenly, there was a ring at the doorbell. Glancing at the clock, Helene frowned. "Who could it be at this hour?"

Margot sighed wearily and got up from the counter. "I'll go find out. Stay here, girls. I'll be back in a minute." Gathering her dressing gown closer to her body, she went to answer the door.

Alexis was sneaking Helene the rest of her whipped

cream when Margot came back to the kitchen. She had a troubled look on her face. "Alexis, it's for you."

"For me?" Alexis cried. "Who is it?"

"Well, dear," Margot replied quietly. "It's your mother."

Seventeen

The Woman in the Iodine Mask

Alexis sat paralyzed as a figure whose face was swathed in bandages walked into the kitchen. The person's only visible features were her eyes—which were surrounded by ugly, yellowing bruises—and her lips, which were puffed twice the size of a normal person's mouth. A thick bandage was taped over the bridge of the nose, and the nostrils were packed with cotton. Her cheeks were covered with cotton pads, too, and the sides of her head were wrapped tightly with bands of gauze. Brown patches of iodine had seeped through much of the bandages. Helene and Margot exchanged horrified glances. If this was Vanessa, what on earth had happened to her?

"Darling," the person croaked from between swollen lips, "I just flew here from Greece. I've been longing to speak with you."

Warily, Alexis got up from her seat and moved closer to the bandaged figure. "Are you *sure* you're my mother?" she asked suspiciously. "You don't sound like her."

The new arrival responded indignantly. "Of course I'm your mother, Alexis. Who else would I be?"

"I don't know," Alexis answered testily. "After all, I haven't seen my mother for ages, and the last time I did, she didn't look anything like this."

The masked woman bowed her head. "I'm supposed to be on total bed rest for the next four weeks to recuperate from my . . . procedure. But I couldn't bear lying around, day after day, knowing I had ruined your summer. I had to come see you."

Just then Helene broke in. "Your timing couldn't be better. Alexis was just getting over the fact that you had abandoned her again. It would have been a shame if you had stayed away and she were actually able to enjoy her summer." Her green eyes flashed with anger.

Margot put a restraining hand on Helene's shoulder. "Helene, please. We should give Alexis and her mother some time alone."

Holding up her hand, Alexis said, "No, I want you both to stay." She then turned back to Vanessa. "Why did you really come here, anyway? To tell me you're broke, and that you need money? To ask me to donate a kidney? You must have a really important reason to visit your only child, whom you haven't seen in three years."

Tears welled in Vanessa's eyes. "I suppose I deserve that," she said. "But I haven't come here to ask for anything, except your forgiveness."

"I'd be more likely to give you a kidney," Alexis said dryly. "Why should I forgive you, after everything you've done to me? Or rather, haven't done for me."

Vanessa pulled out a stool from the counter and perched on top of it. "Alexis, I know I haven't been a good mother," she said. "When I married your father, I saw it as a safety net from poverty. I was a high school dropout. I didn't have any skills. I didn't even have any dreams, apart from finding a rich husband." She took a deep breath. "I never should have gotten married. It wasn't fair to your father. He deserved to marry someone who really loved him. Our marriage was a total mess. But one good thing came out of it. And that was you."

"Exactly when did you come to this startling realization?" Alexis asked coldly.

Vanessa leaned forward pleadingly. "I've always known it, Alexis. Ever since I first held you in my arms. That was the proudest moment of my life."

"If you were so proud of me, why didn't you spend any time with me? Even before the divorce, you were barely around. Everybody knew what a lousy mother you were. That's why Daddy got custody." Despite all of her efforts to stay calm, Alexis's voice was trembling.

"Yeah, and after the divorce, you hardly ever talked to Alexis at all," Helene said. "I know, because I lived with her all those years." She moved to her sister's side and put a protective arm around her shoulders.

"It wasn't that I didn't want to speak to you, darling—I just couldn't," Vanessa said. "I was so ashamed of the way I had behaved, of my failure. I longed to be closer to you, but I never knew what to say when we were together."

"Well, you certainly didn't make much of an effort the last time I visited," Alexis huffed. "You spent the whole time ignoring me. Anytime I came around, you made it abundantly clear that I should go someplace else."

Vanessa bowed her head in shame. "When you came to stay with me that time, I somehow thought you would be this little girl in pigtails, when in reality you had already grown into this stunning young woman. I felt old."

Her voice dripping with sarcasm, Alexis said, "Well, obviously, you've seen the error of your ways and have decided to embrace your true age. That is, after the scars heal from your face-lift."

Margot and Helene winced, and Vanessa probably would have too, if her face hadn't been totally immobilized by bandages. "It was because of my surgery that I realized what a terrible mistake I made. When I invited you to Greece, it was an impulse. I desperately missed you and decided I would make a real effort to repair our relationship before it was too late." Vanessa started tearing up again. Margot passed her a box of Kleenex, which she accepted with gratitude. Dabbing a tissue between the holes in her bandages, she went on. "After I sent the fax I realized that I'd be sailing around the Greek Isles with a beautiful seventeen-year-old who would make me look like an old hag."

Alexis and Helene exchanged looks of contempt, but Margot looked at Vanessa with a sympathetic light in her eye.

"I know it was stupid," Vanessa admitted. "But sometimes it feels like the only reason I've ever gotten anywhere in life is because of my looks. So I scheduled a face-lift with my plastic surgeon, and cancelled your trip."

For the first time, Alexis looked at her with real emotion. "Well, I was better off, anyway. At least I was able to spend the summer with someone who really cares about me." She burrowed deeper into the crook of Helene's arm.

"Alexis, I love you with all my heart. The minute I woke up from surgery, I realized what a terrible thing I had done." Vanessa reached for another tissue.

"And so you think putting on a big mom-and-apple-pie act is going to erase everything that has come before, right?" Alexis said accusingly. "Sorry, I've gone seventeen years without a proper mother. I'm willing to bet I can go seventeen more."

Vanessa's tears began to flow openly. "Alexis, I'm the only mother you've got. Can't you have a little compassion for me?"

At that moment, Alexis's face began to soften just a bit. She remembered the white card she had displayed in her bedroom back home: *The end to suffering can only come through wisdom and compassion.*

She thought back to the days before her parents' divorce, when her mother used to let her play dress-up in her magnificent closet. Then there was the time she had gotten her tonsils out and her mother had slept in the chair beside her hospital bed for the entire time she was there. And the birthday when the whole family had gone to the city to see *Peter Pan.* On the way home, Alexis threw her doll out the car window to see if it could fly like Tinkerbell, and Vanessa forced her infuriated father to pull over on the highway to retrieve it. Alexis remembered the surge of love she had felt when her mother tucked the broken doll back into her arms.

She also thought of Helene, who had given her so much of the unconditional love she'd needed in Vanessa's absence. What would have happened if Helene hadn't shown compassion for all the terrible things she had said and done since coming to Paris? Compassion, Alexis had to admit, really could put an end to suffering. The question remained, though, whether she was brave enough to extend it to her mother.

A hard lump formed in Alexis's throat, but she worked to talk past it. "I'm willing to show you a little compassion, Vanessa, if you're willing to show me some too. After all, I'm a little out of practice having a full-time mother. Do you have any advice on how to make the transition easier?"

Vanessa's swollen lips formed a trembling smile. "You can start by calling me Mom again."

Eighteen

Queen for a Day

The big fashion show was scheduled for July 14—Bastille Day. Helene and Alexis had worked around the clock for weeks preparing for the big event. In the morning, Alexis was still busy in the design studio, altering the exquisite dress her sister was to wear during the show later that evening. Daniel was busy, too, making frantic calls to ensure everything went off without a hitch.

Naturally, Mr. Masterson and Vanessa were a little put out that their daughters were devoting so much time to work. (The Mastersons had generously allowed Vanessa to stay with them so she could spend the rest of the summer with Alexis.) The only time any of them got to see the girls, though, was when they would stumble home from Vedette, tired and irritable from their long hours at the office. Wisely the adults decided to maintain low profiles, as the girls learned to handle so much stress.

Fortunately, Margot was a great help to both Helene and Alexis, offering sage advice on everything from hair and makeup to fittings. When Helene had a terrible acne breakout (i.e., three zits), Margot had taken her to her own private facialist, who was officially retired and only saw a very few clients on an emergency basis. Three treatments later, Helene's skin was as soft and smooth as velvet.

When Alexis ran short of bugle beads and was informed she couldn't get any more for another four weeks, Margot snuck her into the wardrobe department of the movie studio, where they ransacked the shelves for the supplies she needed.

"This must be the only time in history where the wicked stepmother turns into the fairy godmother," Helene remarked when Alexis ran into the kitchen, unloading her booty onto the counter.

Alexis nodded with relief. "If it hadn't been for her, your dress would never have been ready on time."

When the big day finally came, Helene, true to form, was more than a little uncomfortable with all the pomp and circumstance involved with the show. No matter how much Daniel urged her to "just be herself," the Helene she knew was still too used to grabbing the spotlight, not having it trained on her from the beginning.

"Listen to me," he said to Helene a few days before the big event, his voice tinged with exasperation. "When you walk down the runway, don't think of the dozens of

editors and the bank of photographers and Elsa Klensch
staring at you through those thick-rimmed glasses, not to
mention the hundreds of spectators whose eyes will be
poring over you looking for flaws—"

"Daniel!" Helene practically screamed. "You're not
helping!"

"And you're not listening," Daniel insisted. "I said,
don't think of them. They don't exist. Or they are invisi-
ble. However you choose to imagine it. Instead, think of
the people you love, your family, all there to support you,
and feel yourself float down the runway on their love."

"That's just it," Helene said. "Every time I imagine
myself looking down into the crowd for the people I care
about, I see Alexis and my dad and Margot, and Vanessa's
there, and you, too."

"I'll be backstage pinning dresses on models," Daniel
said. "And guzzling coffee by the gallon, and downing
antacids."

Helene ignored this. "And I also see," she pressed on,
"I see . . . Lazlo."

"Lazlo?" Daniel said. "Who is this Lazlo? Tell me
where to find him and I will tie him to a chair at the very
tip of the runway, if that will make you feel better. *Chérie*,
we only have a few days left!"

Helene quickly brought Daniel up to speed on the
Lazlo affair. Well, not so quickly: It took her about two

hours. Finally, after being forced to listen to All the Possible Reasons Lazlo Might Have Dumped Me, Part 17, Daniel glanced at his watch and then said, "If you're so mystified, why don't you just call him and ask?"

Helene recoiled. "Oh, Daniel, I just *couldn't*."

"But you're devastated by it!" Daniel yelled.

"Yes, but I could never admit that to him."

"Because you have too much pride."

Before Helene could come up with a response, Daniel stalked off to his office to make more phone calls. Helene went back to practicing her model's walk. She was starting to get a hang of it, only she still tripped whenever she tried to mount the stairs that had been set up at the end of the runway.

Meanwhile, Alexis was trying to come to terms with the fact that her friendship with Philippe had become decidedly chilly. They'd hardly seen anything of each other since his date with Helene (the morning after Vanessa's arrival, Helene had assured her there hadn't been any sparks between them, and for some strange reason, Alexis was compelled to sing songs from *West Side Story* under her breath). Even though she was disappointed that things had not worked out between Helene and Philippe, she still hoped that she and he would resume their old friendship. But so far, their meetings had been limited to brief hellos at company meetings.

She soon began to realize just how much she had come to look forward to their outdoor lunches and late-night films. Maybe I've made a mistake, Alexis thought for a fleeting moment when she walked past the movie house where he had taken her on their first date. Wait, she thought, was that a date?

The next day, Alexis asked Daniel if the photographers were working on something new.

"No, not exactly, but Philippe is on a special assignment," Daniel said. "Why do you ask?"

"Oh, no reason," she said. Strangely, the knowledge that Philippe wasn't purposely avoiding her—that he was just putting in long hours with some gorgeous model— didn't make her feel any better about the situation.

Fortunately, Helene's dress took a great deal of her time and attention. It was a gorgeous ivory gown, made of silk, with a draped neckline and a mermaid train. Tiny bugle beads were sewn into the bodice, giving it a soft shimmer. A white satin underskirt made the dress cascade like water around the wearer's hips. It was a triumph, and even the demanding Daniel had only words of praise for it.

Still, such an intricate gown required lots of time and effort. Helene was brought in for fittings virtually every day; Alexis was determined that her masterpiece was going to show well on the catwalk. The only relief to having such an engrossing project was that Philippe had put an end to their late evening movies together and it gave her a way to fill the time without him.

Rehearsals for the fashion show began the last week of June. A line of models pranced down the catwalk bearing royal gifts for Helene, who was supposed to play the role of queen. Among the things she received were a jeweled scepter, a pair of glass slippers, and a bouquet of flowers. Only after the last lady-in-waiting turned to model her dress did Helene come down the runway to a fanfare of trumpets.

She would walk to the edge of the platform, turn, and return to the middle of the runway, where a gilt throne would appear, rising up from beneath an underground platform. Helene would then sit on the throne to accept, one by one, the gifts from her ladies-in-waiting. Finally, a male model would come from behind the throne to crown Helene with a glittering tiara.

The mechanics of this setup created all sorts of headaches, especially when the throne failed to rise from the platform due to a broken flywheel. For a few tense hours it looked as though Daniel was ready to call the whole show off. Happily, a workman was eventually able to repair the problem, and rehearsals went smoothly after that. By the time July 14 arrived, everybody was ready to put on the best fashion show Paris had seen in years.

Backstage, Alexis and the other designers were frantically checking each dress to make sure it fit properly. The models were busy jockeying for the best hairdressers and makeup artists. Helene was too nervous to even notice she had hair, much less care who styled it.

Fortunately, Daniel had arranged for the best hair and makeup artists to focus exclusively on his star. Her hair had been dyed dark brown, almost black, and arranged into long, flowing curls down her back. The darkness of her hair contrasted marvelously with her pale skin and green eyes. Her makeup consisted of layers and layers of inky mascara applied to her long, curling eyelashes; a generous coat of bright red lipstick; a dusting of loose powder over her face, neck, and shoulders. Her eyebrows had been plucked into soft arches, giving her a dramatic, imperious look. Daniel came up to survey the effect as the finishing touches were being put on her face.

"You are stunning," he proclaimed after circling her chair. "Absolutely stunning. Like a young Vivien Leigh. You will be, without a doubt, the talk of modeling circles for years to come."

"Thanks," said Helene through chattering teeth. "But wait and see if I get through this show before booking me for any others."

Daniel gave a good-natured laugh. "Just go out there and have a good time. Do you remember your music cue?"

Helene nodded. "'God Save the Queen,' by the Sex Pistols. I'll be ready."

He clapped her on the shoulder. "Good girl. Remember to hold your head high when you're being crowned. Cartier lent us the tiara; it's worth $1.5 million dollars."

She dug her nails into the arms of the chair. "Thanks for telling me," she said sarcastically. "I'm nervous enough without having to worry about getting mugged on the catwalk."

"Don't worry," Daniel reassured her. "I've already arranged for a page to take extra-special care of you this evening. He's promised to guard you with his life." He glanced at his watch. "*Mon dieu!* I'm supposed to introduce the show in five minutes."

"Okay," Helene said weakly. "See you out there. I'll be the one standing stock still on the runway, frozen in terror."

"The applause of the crowd will warm you up, I'm sure," Daniel said distractedly, then strode to the runway.

Alexis came forward. "Hi, honey. I just came to hold your hand until your big entrance." As she said this, Helene grabbed her sister's arm so hard that Alexis was afraid it would snap off. "Hey, watch it!" she yelped. "That's my sewing arm."

All of a sudden, Daniel's voice came booming out over the loudspeaker.

"Ladies and gentlemen, welcome to the launch of Vedette's new clothing line, Fit for a Queen. Some of you may be wondering why a Frenchman like myself would choose such an aristocratic name for a label, especially one that is being launched on Bastille Day." A wave of laughter came from the crowd. "But, I assure you, these clothes have been designed to make all young girls feel like royalty. So with that in mind, it is my great pleasure to introduce my fabulous new fashion line. Enjoy!"

The music swelled, and the ladies-in-waiting began sauntering down the catwalk. Alexis dragged Helene to her feet, putting her into position for her cue. Finally, Helene heard the first crashing chords of her intro music, and stepped onto the runway into a dazzling pool of light.

The crowd gave a loud roar of approval. Hearing the applause, Helene broke out into a warm smile, and glided down the catwalk as if she were floating on a cloud. Mr. Masterson, Margot, and Vanessa were in the front row, right at the base of the runway. Seeing their enthusiasm, she gave a jaunty wink, then pivoted smoothly and made her way to the throne that was rising up from the floor.

One, two, three steps and she was safe in her seat. The ladies-in-waiting came forward. Each one presented her gift, curtsied, and moved to the side. Finally, the moment of truth. Johnny Rotten's voice rose to a howling crescendo over the loud speakers. A page holding a purple pillow with a tiara perched on top came forward. He got down on bended knee and held the pillow up, presenting the crown for Helene's inspection. As the page lifted his face, Helene noticed that his nose had a strange twist . . . almost like . . .

"LAZLO!" she shrieked, jumping up from the throne and nearly sending the tiara flying into the front row— fortunately, Daniel had had the good sense to sew it onto the pillow with a couple of loose stitches. Before she realized what she was doing, the queen threw her arms around the page and they were locked in a passionate kiss.

A fresh roar of approval came up from the crowd. It took a few moments for Helene to remember where she was. Blushing, Helene tried to disentangle herself from Lazlo's embrace. He stopped kissing her, but held firmly to her hand, grinning wickedly. Then, turning to face the crowd, the happy couple gave a deep bow. The music ended. The lights went out. The show was finally over.

They were both backstage before Helene remembered that she hadn't heard from Lazlo in over six weeks. "How come you didn't return any of my e-mails?" she wailed, punching him on the shoulder.

"Because I hadn't received any of them!" he cried in despair. "I installed a new spam blocker on my computer, and it kept deleting your messages as junk mail. At first, I thought that you had stopped writing *me*. By the time I realized what had happened, you had already left for Paris."

Helene threw up her hands. "So why didn't you call me when you found out what happened?"

Exasperated, Lazlo answered, "I did, dozens of times. Your mom gave me your dad's number in Paris. Only every time I called, a man would answer and hang up the phone. Finally, I got so frustrated that I decided to come and see you face-to-face. When I got here, your stepmother told me about the fashion show and—"

"Wait a minute," Helene interrupted. "You called and a man kept hanging up the phone? But why?"

Just then, Mr. Masterson came back stage to congratulate his daughter.

"DADDY!" Helene wailed. "Did you actually hang up the phone every time a boy called for me?"

Mr. Masterson looked distinctly uncomfortable. "Well, the line might have gotten accidentally disconnected a few times. You know how tricky those long-distance calls can be." He paused for a moment and then completely changed tact. "I'm really sorry about that. I promise it won't happen again." He took Lazlo's hand. "It's a pleasure to meet you, young man."

"And you too, sir," Lazlo said sincerely, apparently not holding a grudge about the phone calls.

Helene sighed happily. "Well, I'm glad you're finally here. I can't tell you how much I've missed you."

"If you missed me so much, how come *you* didn't call *me*?" Lazlo demanded.

"Um . . . er . . . uh . . . ," Helene stammered.

"Don't be too hard on the poor girl, Lazlo," Alexis cut in. "If it's any consolation, she hasn't stopped talking about you for six solid weeks!"

Just then, Daniel came over, bearing a huge smile and an overflowing bottle of champagne.

"Daniel!" Helene cried. "I'm sorry I screwed up the big finish. I just got so excited when I saw Lazlo here."

"It went just as I had planned," Daniel said. "When Margot told me that your young friend had arrived in Paris, I just had to include him in the show. Your reunion made for a perfect fairy tale ending, did it not?"

"It did," Helene said happily, squeezing Lazlo's hand. Glancing over her shoulder, she said, "Speaking of fairy tale endings . . ."

Philippe stepped from behind a clothes rack.

"Philippe? What are you doing here?" Alexis gasped. "Daniel told me you were out on an important assignment."

He nodded. "I was. Actually, it was Helene's idea. You see, she prepared a whole dossier on it." Reaching into his leather jacket, he pulled out a manila envelope and handed it to Alexis. Confusedly, she reached inside and pulled out a photo of herself, with a typewritten note attached:

Name: Alexis Worth, aka "The Designing Woman"
Height: 5'6"
Hair: Long and luxurious
Eyes: For Yours Only

Your Mission (Should You Choose to Accept It): Despite her gold-digging act, Alexis is actually a talented, intelligent girl who is in the market for a loving, attentive boyfriend. Do not undertake this assignment unless you fully intend to give her the love, affection, and happiness she truly deserves.

Philippe looked at her. "What do you say? May I stamp this assignment 'Mission Accomplished'?"

Alexis's eyes brimmed. Without saying a word, she leaned and kissed him with a passion she never knew she possessed. Safe in his warm embrace, she felt as if she'd finally reached nirvana.

Nineteen

Liberté, Egalité, Sororité

"This is one place we couldn't miss while we were in Paris," Alexis said, as Helene nodded in agreement. They were standing at the Liberty Flame, just at the base of the Pont de l'Alma, a few feet from where Princess Diana had been killed. The statue had originally been built as a testament to Franco-American friendship. After the accident, though, people had turned it into a makeshift shrine to the beloved princess.

Alexis carried a posy of white sweetheart roses, while Helene had brought a bouquet of colorful anemones. They both came forward and laid the flowers at the base of the statue, which was covered with photographs of the late princess as well as handwritten messages from people all over the world.

Slowly they rounded the base of the statue so they could view all the photos people had taped there. They saw pictures of the princess from every phase of her life: as a shy young bride, a happy newlywed, a proud mother, and a social activist. Rounding the column, it struck both girls afresh how many different facets there were to such a remarkable woman. There was a picture of an aloof, regal Diana in a tiara. Another photo showed her dressed in a simple sweater and jeans, hugging her sons with evident delight. Still another had her dressed in a sexy black cocktail dress, surrounded by a crowd of admirers. Finally Alexis spotted a picture of Diana and Fergie, doubled over with laughter. She slipped her hand into Helene's and gave it a tight squeeze. Helene squeezed back and gave a sad sigh.

Gazing at a particularly lovely photo of the princess, in which her big, blue eyes seemed to take up half her face, Helene said, "She was so beautiful, but that just seemed to make her life even more miserable. Everybody was so busy idolizing her, they forgot to treat her like a human being." She paused. "You know, I'm starting to think that being gorgeous isn't all that it's cracked up to be. Beauty just presents its own set of problems."

Laughing ruefully, Alexis said, "And marrying a rich man doesn't solve anything, either. As far as Diana was concerned, it seemed to actually hold her back, in lots of ways. It was as though all that money was always being held over her head. I bet a lot of women who depend on men for money suffer from low-self esteem, just like she did."

"After the divorce, she seemed like she became a lot more confident," Helene observed. "Who knows how far she would have gone if she hadn't died?"

Alexis nodded soberly. "It just goes to show, you can't waste any time trying to win other people's approval. You have to find what you want from life and go for it."

"Yeah, but that attitude can be taken too far," Helene protested. "I mean, you can justify all sorts of behavior by putting your own interests first."

"Not necessarily," Alexis said slowly. "Not if you learn to develop compassion. It's funny, but I've found that when I behave compassionately toward others, my interests and theirs usually coincide. Like giving my mother a second chance. Turns out that it was the best thing I could have ever done for myself, too. I feel ten pounds lighter. I guess I didn't realize how much anger I had been carrying around."

"Don't forget how you took compassion on me and Philippe and set us up on a date," Helene teased.

Alexis flushed. "Well, that *did* end up benefiting everybody, didn't it? If I hadn't gotten you guys together, Philippe would have never gotten the courage to confess his feelings for me. And you wouldn't have had the pleasure of playing matchmaker."

Helene laughed. "Who could argue with that logic?"

Twenty

Le Déjeuner sur l'Herbe

It was Alexis and Helene's last week in Paris, and Philippe and Lazlo were taking them to the Tuileries for a picnic.

Mercifully the hot summer sun wasn't nearly as strong as it had been in past weeks, so the girls felt cool and comfortable in their light clothing. Alexis was wearing a pink top and flowered cotton skirt, while Helene sported a white sundress. Philippe had on his customary T-shirt and jeans, and Lazlo wore khakis and a polo shirt.

"It's such a relief not to be working anymore!" Helene exclaimed as they headed for a lush clump of trees. "I'll never envy models again. So much of it is standing around, waiting for lights to be shifted or hair to be fixed."

Staggering beneath the weight of the picnic basket, Lazlo managed to gasp, "Was Daniel angry when you told him you didn't want to be the new face of Vedette after all?" He dropped the wicker basket into a patch of shade, and it thudded as it hit the ground.

Helene giggled and began unpacking the food. "No, I think he was relieved. He was always having to give me pep talks so I could relax in front of the camera. Besides, once Margot volunteered to take over, he dropped me like a hot potato."

Alexis clutched her heart and feigned a coronary. "Can it be possible? Is my sister actually *glad* to have a stepmother?"

Helene grabbed a roll and threw it at her sister's head. It bounced off onto a nearby walking path, much to the delight of a toy poodle that was just passing by. "Don't be dumb. I don't feel the least bit competitive with Margot. As far as I'm concerned, she can have the limelight. I've got all I need to be happy, right here." She gave Lazlo a quick, noisy kiss.

"I certainly hope you find other things to make you happy, too, before we leave Paris," Alexis said sarcastically. "I don't think I could take another year of 'I miss Lazlo' . . . 'that reminds me of Lazlo' . . . 'this is no good without Lazlo.'"

Philippe laughed delightedly at Alexis's imperson-ation of Helene.

Helene and Lazlo, though, were not as amused. "What's wrong with her missing me?" Lazlo demanded to know. "You have to admit, I'm quite a remarkable guy."

Surveying him wryly, Philippe muttered, "I'll say."

Helene ignored him. "Besides, I've grown a lot this summer. Ever since becoming a model, I realized that all the admiration and adulation in the world doesn't amount to squat. That happiness comes from *within*." She crunched an apple contentedly.

Lazlo nodded sagely. "I'm glad you've said that, my dear, because it makes it much easier to say what I'm about to tell you."

Helene looked up in alarm, her mouth half-filled with apple. "What, Lazlo?"

"I'll be incommunicado for the next twelve months or so. You see, I'm going on a trip to the deserts of Africa, and I won't have much access to e-mail."

"You're kidding," Helene whispered. The color had drained out of her face, and the apple fell out of her slackened hand.

"Gotcha," Lazlo said, causing Alexis and Philippe to fall about in laughter.

"Very funny!" Helene said huffily, picking up her apple and wiping it off on her dress. "You all should have your own comedy show!" With that, she stormed off across the lawn, with Lazlo chasing after her.

"Helene, wait up!" he yelled. She kept running at full speed a good thirty seconds before finally slowing her pace.

"Well, what do you want?" she asked frostily when he finally caught up to her, panting heavily.

Moving to block her path, he said, "I'm sorry I teased you back there. Really, I'm so glad you missed me as much as I missed you."

"Do you really mean it?" Helene asked softly.

Wrapping his arms around her, he murmured, "Yes, I really mean it." They kissed, softly at first, then more and more passionately. Finally, he broke away. "But Helene, it isn't right that we're so miserable when we're apart. Alexis is right: The fact is, we live on separate continents. We have to find things to sustain us while we're away from each other."

Helene nodded miserably. "I know. It's just so hard, when I don't know when I'll ever see you again."

Tilting her chin up, he said, "Well, maybe this will help. My schoolmaster tells me I have an aptitude for business. Says that the best business schools are in America too."

"Lazlo," Helene shrieked. "You don't mean . . ."

"Yes, there's a very good possibility that I'll be attending college in the States. That is, provided I pass my O levels this coming year. So, do you think it will be easier to enjoy your final year of school more, knowing there's a chance we'll be closer once it's over?"

Helene bit her lip. "I've got to try. Gosh, I feel so stupid for getting hung up on a guy this way. I mean, I'm seventeen years old! I should be going out to parties, having fun, meeting people . . ."

Lazlo nodded. "So should I. And we will do those things, just as we did last year. Only this time, we'll be able to do it without wondering when we'll ever see each other again. Let's make a firm resolve to meet over summer holidays next year. And if either us changes our mind, we'll just tell the other, openly and honestly. Agreed?"

Helene smiled. "Agreed. But I don't think my feelings are going to change. Not if my present feelings are any indication."

He gave her another long, lingering kiss. "I don't expect my feelings to change either. Now, having said all that, don't you think we owe it to each other to make the most of our time in Paris? I mean, you've been here six weeks and I'll bet you haven't even seen where Marie Antoinette was guillotined, have you?"

Sadly, Helene shook her head.

"Outrageous!" Lazlo fumed. "Well, I'll soon remedy that. We'll go first thing tomorrow. Don't forget to bring your camera."

Snuggling deeper into his arms, Helene murmured, "Oh, Lazlo, you think of everything, don't you?"

Meanwhile, Alexis and Philippe were poking at the picnic food. Somehow, neither of them was very hungry. He sat with his back against a tree, and she lay with her head on his lap. Playing with a lock of her long hair, he said, "Alexis, this summer has been a dream come true for me. I can't bear to think of you going back to America."

Alexis sighed. "For me too. I've never felt this way about anybody before. It's like something out of a movie, only better. Because it's real."

He leaned to kiss her. "I won't be able to go to the cinema anymore without thinking of you."

"And I won't be able to use my pinking shears anymore without thinking of you." They both laughed, until Alexis sat up. "Seriously, Philippe. Living with Helene, I've seen how difficult long-distance relationships are. It would be a mistake to put our lives on hold just because we're living so far apart. I think we should agree to see other people once the summer is over."

Philippe began ripping tufts of grass from the lawn. Finally, after a few minutes of silence, he gave a long, slow nod. "You're right," he said quietly. "I don't want our relationship to be a source of unhappiness, *chérie*. But I can't help but feel that when the summer ends, we will be giving up something that can never be recaptured."

Alexis smiled softly and fought to keep back her tears. "Well," she said, giving him a deep kiss, "we'll always have Paris."

Gillian McKnight is the author of the popular *To Catch a Prince*, to which *The Frog Prince* is the sequel. She holds an MFA in creative writing from the New School and is currently working on an adult novel set in the west. She divides her time between Brooklyn, NY, and Amherst, MA.